SKIPPER

Books by Paige Dixon

LION ON THE MOUNTAIN
SILVER WOLF
THE YOUNG GRIZZLY
SUMMER OF THE WHITE GOAT
THE LONER: THE STORY OF A WOLVERINE
MAY I CROSS YOUR GOLDEN RIVER?
PROMISES TO KEEP
THE SEARCH FOR CHARLIE
PIMM'S CUP FOR EVERYBODY
SKIPPER

SKIPPER

by
Paige Dixon

ATHENEUM 1980 NEW YORK

LIBRARY OF CONGRESS CATALOGING IN PUBLICATION DATA

Dixon, Paige Skipper.

SUMMARY: Hoping to ease the pain of his brother's
death, Skipper sets off for North Carolina
in search of the father he has never known.
A sequel to "May I cross your golden river."
[1. Death—Fiction. 2. Brothers and sisters—Fiction]
I. Title. PZ7.C814Sk [Fic] 79-10420
ISBN 0-689-30706-3

Copyright © 1979 by Paige Dixon
Published simultaneously in Canada by
McClelland & Stewart, Ltd.
Manufactured by The Book Press,
Brattleboro, Vermont
Designed by Mary M. Ahern
First Printing September 1979
Second Printing July 1980

To the Real Matt

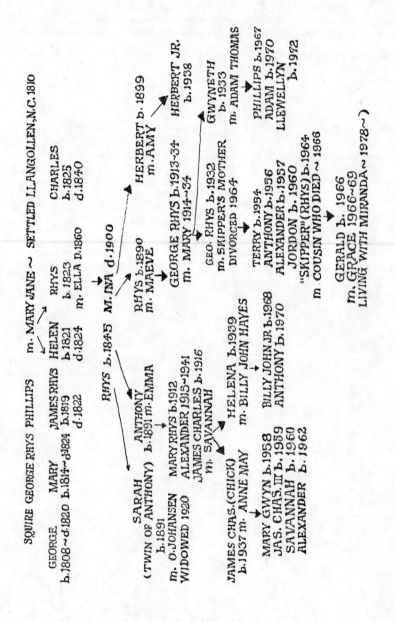

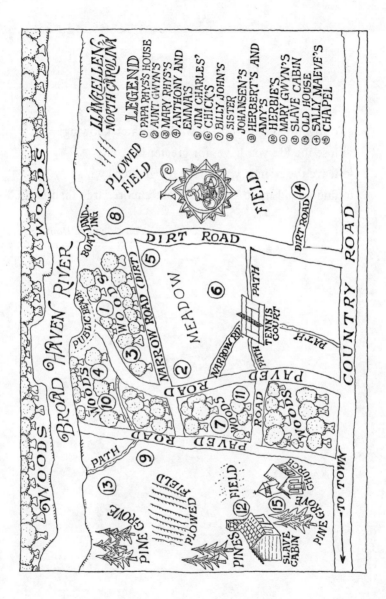

LLANGELLEN,
North Carolina

LEGEND
① PAPA RHYS'S HOUSE
② AUNT GWYN'S
③ MARY RHYS'S
④ ANTHONY AND
   EMMA'S
⑤ JIM CHARLES'
⑥ CHICK'S
⑦ BILLY JOHN'S
⑧ SISTER
   JOHANSEN'S
⑨ HERBERT'S AND
   AMY'S
⑩ HERBIE'S
⑪ MARY GWYN'S
⑫ SLAVE CABIN
⑬ OLD HOUSE
⑭ SALLY MAEVE'S
⑮ CHAPEL

WOODS

BROAD HAVEN RIVER

WOODS

PLOWED
FIELD

BOAT LAND-
ING

⑧

PUBLIC BEACH

WOODS
①

WOODS
④

WOODS
⑩

DIRT ROAD

NARROW ROAD (DIRT)

⑤

③

②

MEADOW

⑥

NARROW RD.

PATH

TENNIS
COURT

PATH

PAVED
ROAD

FIELD

⑭

DIRT ROAD

COUNTRY ROAD

PATH

⑦

WOODS
⑪

PAVED ROAD

PAVED
ROAD

WOODS

PATH

⑨

PLOWED FIELD

PINES

FIELD
⑫

⑮

PINE GROVE

PORCH

SLAVE
CABIN

PINE GROVE

⑬

WOODS

PINE GROVE

— TO TOWN

"To love the earth you know, for greater knowing:
to lose the life you have, for greater life:
to leave the friends you loved, for greater loving:
to find a land more kind than home, more large than earth."

You Can't Go Home Again
Thomas Wolfe

SKIPPER

first

The June sun was warm on Skipper's back as he lay stretched out on the grass beside his brother Jordan's grave. He could smell the lilacs his mother had left, and he heard the distant sound of the caretaker's lawnmower. Cicero, Jordan's Scottie dog, was sprawled on the grass beside him, lifting his head now and then to snap at a lazy fly. Summer was almost here. Skipper thought of fishing and put the thought quickly out of his mind with the little flick of pain that such thoughts brought. Fishing had always included Jordan. Sometimes his older brothers Alex and Tony were along, but he couldn't remember a time when he had gone fishing without Jordan. He reached out and touched the cool marble headstone.

"Tony and Em took Mrs. Ricker to the retirement home

yesterday," he said aloud. "She's been so lonesome since Mr. Ricker died, and she really can't handle that house, with her arthritis. She gave Em the little dog you gave her. It's a nice home, Jordie. Alex checked it out very carefully."

He sat up, and Cicero lifted his head in inquiry. "I went to see the Rickers three or four times after you left us. Remember what super doughnuts she makes? She really thought a lot of you." He looked up at the cloudless sky, where a small plane moved slowly and doggedly toward the mountains. "She's awful lonesome without Mr. Ricker." He sighed heavily. "But she said, 'I've stopped crying. Nobody cries forever.' That's what she said. Tony told me. 'Nobody cries forever.' I guess Tony was trying to tell me something. He usually is. They all think I spend too much time thinking about you." He laughed. "Man, what would they say if they knew how often I come out here and talk to you! And if they knew about the journal I keep that's like really one long letter to you. Alex has already asked me a million questions: Do I dream about you? (I don't.) Do I daydream in school and is that why my grades are down? Do I still see my friends?" He rubbed Cicero's car. "I heard Alex tell Mom that I'm mourning too long. Did you know there's some kind of time limit on mourning? I guess it's written down somewhere, taken off a computer, you know? 'Mourning, limits of: for mother mourning son, 62 days allowed, not counting nights. For older brothers: 33½ days, not counting nights. For youngest brother: 36 days, not counting nights.' So I've broken the rule. I'm into my fifth month. So are the rest of them, if you want to know, Jordie, only they bottle it up, hide it better. But I hear Mom crying at night . . ."

He stopped, swallowing the unexpected tears that still threatened him when he wasn't watchful. He got to his feet.

4

"Maybe the word isn't mourning so much as remembering—
and trying to understand." He stood looking down at the
neatly cut grass. "Trying to understand, figure it out. Remember the night up at Estes Park, after you knew you were
going to die, and we talked about the stars? About Bode's
Law, and the patterns that exist in the universe? The way I
look at it, this has to be some kind of pattern too. All I'm
trying to do is find out what it is." Unseeingly he watched
the small figure of the groundskeeper on the far side of the
small country cemetery. "I keep thinking that our old man
must be some kind of clue to our patterns. You just barely
remembered him, I never saw him. He's just a name on my
ten-dollar birthday check every year. I think I'm going to
look him up. Maybe if I could get him out here . . . This
summer. You told me to go see him sometime, do you
remember? All right, sire, I fly to fulfill your command."
Sometimes the only way to keep from bursting into tears was
to pretend to be funny. One of the last things Jordan had
said to him was to keep the family's spirits up, tell them
jokes. And he had promised he would.

Skipper whistled to Cicero and started for the road where
his ten-speed bike was parked. He took the long way home
to avoid the campus where his mother taught. If she saw him
coming from the direction of the Baseline, she would guess
right away that he had been out to the cemetery again, and
it upset her. They didn't understand that it wasn't morbid—
it really wasn't. If he went off and sat on top of one of the
Flatiron Mountains and said he was thinking about God and
the universe, or Zen, or his own soul, they'd nod under-
standingly and say, "He's at that age." But because it was
his brother who was the focus of his attention, they thought
he was being weird.

5

Cicero's bark reminded him that he was pedaling too fast. He still hadn't gotten used to the ease and speed of his new bike. His mother had given it to him on his birthday last winter, but he hadn't been able to ride it then with all the snow they'd had. He looked back at Cicero, whose short legs were pounding up and down like pistons. "Come on there, Furred Bird, fly!"

Tomorrow the whole family was coming for dinner—his sister Terry and her husband, and his brothers, Tony and Alex, and Alex's wife. He supposed Emily would come too. There seemed to be a big thing going between Tony and Em, which he did not quite approve of. She lived next door to them, when she wasn't in veterinary school in Fort Collins, and he had always thought she would marry Jordan. Once when he had mentioned it, she had smiled and rumpled his hair and said, "That thought seems to have been in everyone's mind except Jordan's and mine. If you must know, Skip, I've had my sights set on Tony since I was in rompers."

"What are rompers?"

"A small-child garment worn before you were born."

He liked Em, and it would be nice to have her for a sister-in-law, if it came to that, but he still had a funny feeling that she belonged to Jordan and it wasn't right for her to settle for Tony.

"But what do I know," he said to Cicero. "You and me, we're the runts of the litter. We don't know from nothin'."

second

They were all there for Sunday dinner, most of them gathered in the living room as Skipper came down the stairs. He had slept late, tired after working till midnight at the supermarket. They called out to him, and Tony, who was standing at the bottom of the stairs trying to get his pipe going, looked over, frowning, and said in a low voice, "You're limping again."

"I am not." It annoyed Skipper when Tony said that. He was sure it wasn't true.

"You were. And you're hanging onto the bannister."

Skipper pulled his hand back from the bannister as if it were hot. Tony said he was unconsciously assuming the limp and some of the other habits that Jordan had been forced into in his illness.

7

"You're out of your mind," he said to Tony, and went into the living room to say hello to his sister's husband Pat, and his brother Alex and his wife.

Alex's wife Jennifer kissed him. "Hi, love. Long time no see."

Skipper gave her an extravagant hug. "Alex, do you mind if Jennifer and I elope? Like maybe Tuesday?"

"Make it Saturday," Alex said, "and I'll go with you."

Em came in from the kitchen, and she kissed Skipper too.

"What's with all this kissing?" Tony said. "I don't get kissed like that."

"You aren't as cute as I am," Skipper said.

His mother joined them, pushing her hair back from her forehead and wiping her face with her handkerchief. "That kitchen is hot!"

"Well, if you only wouldn't get all the work done before we get here," Em said, "we'd help." She smiled affectionately at Mrs. Phillips.

"That is an illogical statement," Skipper said. "The kitchen would be hotter, not cooler, with the addition of other warm bodies."

"Anyway it smells wonderful," Pat said.

Mrs. Phillips smiled at him. "How was the service? I'm sorry I didn't get there."

He shrugged. "Fair to middlin'. This weather tempts people up into the mountains. In fact, my wife's been trying to talk me into going up to Estes Park for a few days, before the tourists invade."

Skipper looked at him quickly. He had spent a few days with Jordan in Estes Park last Thanksgiving, when the town was frozen in and hardly anyone was there. It had been the happiest time of his life, in spite of his grief at the knowledge

8

that his brother was dying. They had come close together in those few days in a way he would never forget. He would never go to Estes Park again because he wanted to keep that memory exactly as it was.

Terry came downstairs carrying her baby, five-month-old Jordan. The baby had been born in time for his uncle Jordan to stand up in church as his godfather. Now he was plump and alert with long-lashed blue eyes that looked amused.

"Hey, Little J.," Skipper said, "how you doin'?" He took the baby from Terry and hugged him. The others called the child "Jordan" or "Jordie," but although he loved him so much it made him ache, Skipper could not bring himself yet to call him by his brother's name. For him there was only one Jordie.

They went in to dinner.

"I really love the new table," Jennifer said.

They all spoke of it as if it were simply a new piece of furniture, but Skipper was sure they knew why his mother had bought it. No matter how she tried to rearrange the place settings on the old oak table, there always was the place that Jordan had sat at, the empty place that everyone was aware of. The new table was oval. Places were not so clearly defined, and Jordan had never sat there.

Skipper suspected from the worried glance his mother gave him once or twice that she had seen him or seen his bike at the cemetery. Or maybe just seen him riding down the Baseline. She would get together with Tony and Alex, and they would worry about him. He hated their worrying, hated to think he caused them added concern, but also hated it on his own account. He wanted to be left alone to think of Jordan in his own way. But if she had discussed it with the other boys, no one said anything. Later, he thought, later one of them will take me aside and say, "Look, Skip, there's a time for grief and a time to put it behind you. You're young, your life is ahead of you . . ." and so on, blah-blah-blah. They meant well, but Skipper hated it.

He had been intending to tell them about his plan, but after dinner he kept putting it off. It wasn't going to be easy. There'd be a thousand objections, especially from his mother. She still thought of him as the baby. Only Jordan had finally understood that he was growing up.

He started to bring it up after the girls finished with the dishes, but just then Alex went outside with his mother to talk about the vegetable garden she was putting in.

"Mom looks tired," Tony said.

Somehow feeling accused, Skipper said, "You'd be tired too if you had all those idiot students to cope with. They call her up all hours. 'Mrs. Phillips, I can't think of a subject for my term paper.' 'Mrs. Phillips, is "To be or not to be" an infinitive phrase and anyway what does it *mean* exactly, allegorically speaking?' "

They all laughed. Terry put young Jordan down on the floor and he began to pull himself across the rug.

Pat leaned forward to rescue the quilt that was folded across the end of the couch as the baby tugged at one end of it.

"The quick crab catches the crazy quilt," Skipper said.

"He does move like a crab," Terry said, "sideways, in a kind of scuttle."

Mrs. Phillips and Alex came into the room and at that moment Pat asked Skipper the question that gave him his cue.

"What are you going to do this summer, Skip?"

They all looked at him. Skipper started to speak. His voice

10

broke, and they laughed. Usually he didn't mind, but just now it irritated him.

"Anybody'd think you guys were born with deep bass voices," he said. "Born six feet tall. Born free."

"What's eating you?" Tony said.

"I was going to tell you what I'm going to do this summer. Pat did ask."

"So tell."

"I'm going back east to look up my father."

If he had said he was going to join the Foreign Legion, the effect would have been less startling. There was absolute silence except for the sharp sound of his mother's gasp.

Then Tony said, "That's not funny, kiddo."

"It wasn't meant to be. It's not a joke."

Terry said, "You mean you really want to do it, Skip?"

"I mean I'm really going to do it."

Alex and Tony exchanged glances. Tony said, "How do you plan to get there?"

"I plan to ride my very splendid ten-speed bike." He was trying not to look at his mother.

"No," she said, "no, Skipper. Absolutely not."

He made himself look at her. "I'm sorry, Mom. I really have to."

And the barrage of objections that he had expected began, from everyone except Terry, who was listening intently.

JOURNAL ENTRY: You wouldn't believe the opposition. They thought of things even I hadn't thought of.

MOM: "If you're not killed by a car, you'll be killed by some crazy person."

TONY: "You can't ride a bike on interstates. You'd be arrested."

11

ME: "So I'll go country roads."

ALEX: "Do you realize it would take you most of the summer just to get there and back?"

ME: "I can do seventy-five miles a day."

ALEX: "Day after day after day?"

JENNIFER: "Skipper *dear,* it will be sizzling hot and they have tornadoes and heaven knows what."

PAT: "It really isn't advisable."

ME: "So who asked for advice?"

EM: "Let's say you're in the middle of Kansas and night is coming on and you have a flat tire."

ME: "So I go to sleep in the nearest wheatfield and fix the tire in the morning."

Jordie, it got really hot and heavy, with Mom bursting into tears and everybody looking at me as if I'm Super-Monster. And suddenly, in a quiet voice, Terry speaks up.

TERRY: "I think everybody's being awfully emotional about this. It's really not worth it, is it? Everybody's reacting as if Skipper is still ten years old, but he isn't. To all intents and purposes he's grown-up. He grew up when Jordan died. He's got to look for answers in his own way, just as the rest of us did." (Then she looks at me.) "Skipper, I don't think it's terribly practical to think of riding your bike all the way. Have you thought about taking a train to the east coast, and packing your bike along in the baggage car?"

ME: "I hadn't thought of that." (By this time I am about to burst into tears myself, out of pure gratitude at being stuck up for by my sis.)

SIS: "Why don't you look into that possibility? Or even the

12

Greyhound Bus. You could take your bike apart and box it up and take it along, I think."

ME: "I'll look into it."

And on that note the conference ended.

JOURNAL: One week later. I don't know whether Mom or I has been trying harder to understand the other one's point of view. I almost wish she wouldn't try so hard. She gets pale and tight-lipped and gives me this bleak smile and says, "I do see, Skipper. I do see you need to do something." And I gulp and say, "Mom, I don't want to worry you or anything. It's just that . . ." And she says, "I know." But maybe neither of us is getting anywhere.

JOURNAL: One week and one day later. We all foregathered today at the abode of our sister, and hallelujah, the wind has shifted. Now everybody is full of constructive suggestions. I suspect Terry has been brainwashing them, separately and collectively. The consensus is: 1.) that Skipper should not travel that long way on his bike. 2.) that since Tony has an appointment for an interview at a school in Washington, D.C., on June 26, said Skipper should fly with him, shipping bike by air cargo, and then take off on his own. I said I didn't have plane fare, but that was waved aside. Collectively they will take care of that. Well, it's all right with me. I have no burning desire to pedal three or four thousand miles (round trip) if I can fly. So the situation seems to be, as of this writing, "I'm Skipper. Fly me to Washington."

JOURNAL: June 20. I am both excited and scared. It turns out that it wasn't because she didn't want to talk about our

13

dear father that Mom has always been such a fountain of non-information—it's because she really doesn't know much, aside from what he was like while he lived with her, which was, I gather, amiable, unreliable, fond of shooting his salary in a crap game, spoiled, thoughtless, not unkind in any deliberate way. She knows that his parents owned an antique shop somewhere in Charleston, S.C., and are dead. She knows he had some grandparents and a thousand cousins somewhere in North Carolina, who disapproved of him, and who are probably by now deceased (the grandparents at least.) She knows he had one sister, possibly more. He was apparently the black sheep, our father. Alex is the last one who got a birthday check from him, and it was postmarked Chapel Hill, North Carolina, and drawn on a Durham, North Carolina, bank, so obviously he is no longer in Bangor, Maine. The lad gets around. Yours truly is going to have to be a private eye to even find the guy. Oh, well, I can enjoy the scenery. They say North Carolina is nice. Mom thinks the family has been there for generations. I know Alex thinks the change "will do me good." Get my mind off things. *Et cetera.* He took me aside and put his arm around my shoulders and said, "But, look, kiddo, don't expect to find Jordan." I said, "Don't be silly." And he said, "But that's what you keep looking for." And he recited something to me I think he had memorized for the occasion, from a man named Rabbi Chaim Stern: "Life and death alike are mysterious. We journey through a country dimly seen by the uncertain light of thought and feeling, and death is undiscovered territory, a land without report." Oh, Jordie, what *am* I looking for? What will I find? I just hope it won't be nothing at all.

14

third

JOURNAL: Washington really blew my mind. Tony and I gawked at the White House and walked Pennsylvania Avenue, climbed Washington Monument, said hi to Tom Jefferson, and nearly fell into the reflecting pool trying to get a good look at the Lincoln Memorial. Tony took me to dinner at the hotel where he's staying and then put me and my trusty bike on a bus for Chapel Hill. The guy in the next seat was very nice, and he told me a little what it's like to be black in the South. He's from Charleston and he goes to a black college in Maryland. Really a cool guy. He's on the basketball team there, so I told him I play at home, and we shot the breeze about basketball and sports in general. Then I fell asleep. I've been too excited to sleep since we left Denver.

We got to Chapel Hill next day and I am now holed up in a motel from which I shall conduct my detective work. There is no George Rhys Phillips in either the Chapel Hill or the Durham phone book. I had fried ham and grits for breakfast; fried chicken, blackeyed peas, rice, and hush puppies for lunch. I may just stay here and eat myself to death. Called Mom and reversed the charges. She said check public school administrative offices, and if no luck, check *Who's Who* in the library. One of the Phillipses, she had just remembered hearing, is or was a historian, fairly big in these parts. Biography might give address. Nice to have an educated mother.

fourth

When Skipper had called the Chapel Hill, Durham, and county school administration offices with no results, he rode his bike over to the campus. He liked Chapel Hill. The pines made him homesick. At the library he found *Who's Who in the South* in the reference room. There was no listing for a North Carolina Phillips. He left the reference room and was looking at a science fiction collection when it occurred to him that the Phillips historian might be old and no longer active. He went back and started pulling down volumes dated earlier. In the 1965–66 book he found:

PHILLIPS, JOHN CHARLES, historian; b. Fayetteville, N.C., Apr. 2, 1916. S. Anthony Rhys and Emma (Baldwin) Phillips; B.A., Univ. No. Carolina, 1938; Ph.d., Harvard Univ., 1942. Prof. history: Duke Univ. 1942–present: M. Savannah Jones. Children: John Charles III, Helena. Mem. Nat'l. Assoc. Historians, Modern Lang. Assoc., Phi Beta Kappa, Sigma Nu. Author numerous textbooks and historical accounts including: *A Southerners' Look at the War Between the States, Life of Stonewall Jackson, The Welsh in the North Carolina Piedmont.* Contrib. articles to historical journals. Home: Llangollen, N.C."

The very first day, and he had a lead! He got down a big atlas and turned to North Carolina. It took some squinting to find Llangollen. It appeared in very fine print, in the southeastern part of the state. It must be about big enough for four pecan trees and a couple of houses, Skipper thought. He copied down all the data on Phillips, John Charles, and marked the location on his own road map.

Old Private Eye Phillips! Success guaranteed within the hour. He rode around the town for a while, peering at the names on mailboxes, hoping to see George R. Phillips, but there were no Phillipses. He was chased by a large German shepherd and yapped at by a miniature poodle, was given "Good Morning" by nearly everyone he met. He stopped to look at the enormous white flowers on a tree with glossy leaves. An old lady carrying a net bag full of groceries came by and he asked her what it was.

"You must be a Yankee," she said, "not to know magnolias."

"I'm never sure what a Yankee is," Skipper said. "I'm from Colorado, near Denver."

18

"Oh yes," she said. "Hilly country."

Skipper smiled. "Very hilly. Would you like me to carry your bag for you?"

He put the bag in the carrier and walked his bicycle beside her along a path into a stand of tall longleaf pines. Deep in the grove they came to her house, a small log cabin with gardenia bushes around the door. She invited him in and gave him iced tea.

"What a super cabin," he said, looking at the floor-to-ceiling bookcases, the big fieldstone fireplace, the comfortable furniture, the good stereo.

"My son built it for me when I retired. He brought some of those fireplace stones all the way from Bat Valley. Would you like a piece of corn bread? I'm afraid I don't keep much on hand that would tempt a young man. I'm very ancient, you know."

"What did you retire from?" He took the piece of buttered corn bread she brought him and thanked her. "You've got a lot of books."

"I taught English at Sweet Briar for more years than I can remember."

"What's Sweet Briar?"

She looked a little shocked. "It's a very good women's college in Virginia."

"Oh, you'll have to excuse my ignorance. I've never been anywhere or heard of anything."

She gave him a smile that lit up her face. "But here you are."

Rather to his surprise he heard himself telling her why he was here. He even told her about Jordan, a topic he avoided completely at home.

"So you're really a Tarheel, just slightly removed." She smiled that enchanting smile again. "I knew you were a nice boy. I know of the Phillips family, of course. They say, you know, that all North Carolinians are cousins, though that's a slight exaggeration. I know John Charles Phillips by reputation but I don't recall that we've met. He would be so much younger than I am."

"*Who's Who's* says he's sixty-three."

"And I'm ninety-one—a bit of a gap there. But if you get to Llangollen, you'll surely find plenty of kin."

He left her reluctantly after a half-hour of pleasant talk. She was a nice lady, and he had enjoyed talking about home and family. On an impulse he said, "My brother Jordan would have liked you. He had an elderly lady friend that he was real fond of."

"That's the boy who died?"

"Yes." It was still hard to say "yes" to that.

"And you've come because of him."

"Well, I want to see my father."

"Finding family helps. But, child, bury your dead." She put her hand lightly on his wrist.

"What do you mean?"

"Let them go, the dead."

"You mean forget Jordan? I couldn't ever do that."

"No, no, not forget. One never forgets. But let him go and look to your own life, it's all ahead of you." She leaned forward, studying his face. "You don't understand me."

"Not really."

"If he had gone to China, or if he'd flown off in the space ship *Enterprise,* you'd not be carrying him about with you as you're doing now. He's gone on a farther journey, but put him down, child. Look to your future."

20

He pedaled slowly along the path, bumping over roots. A bird with a vivid red breast flew past his head, and somewhere a woodpecker kept up a noisy hammering. He had enjoyed the old lady, but he wished they hadn't gotten into all that right at the end. It made him feel depressed. He came back into the main street and had barbecued beef on a bun in a small, cool restaurant. It was so good, he had another, and felt better.

He checked out of the motel and started south. Obeying his brothers' instructions, he stayed on country roads, although they were less direct. The sun grew hot, and he was glad he had remembered to fill his canteen with ice water. As the hours went by, he was grateful for the comfortable saddle he had hated to spend his money for. He laughed, thinking of his outrage the day he came home to find that Tony had removed the saddle from the bike, soaked it in neat's-foot oil and was pounding on it with a ball peen hammer. It was the best way, Tony tried to explain, to soften up a saddle so you could ride indefinitely without discomfort. At the time Skipper had thought Tony had ruined it, but now he knew his brother was right: the saddle was as soft and flexible as a chunk of foam rubber.

He rode until dark and then stopped at a small motel in a country town. Left to his own wishes, he might have camped out, but his mother was convinced that North Carolina was crawling with poisonous snakes. He'd come across two snakes killed by cars, but they were harmless king snakes. It was mosquitoes, not snakes, that made him glad to spend the night inside. While he registered, still slapping and scratching, the woman at the desk sold him a can of Off.

"Spray yourself good, and you won't have trouble. Mosquitoes purely hate that stuff."

21

On her advice he ate at a tiny restaurant across the road, where he had his first taste of fried catfish, with coleslaw and hush puppies and two pieces of sweet potato pie. He slept that night, only dimly aware of a smashing thunderstorm and high winds.

fifth

It was early afternoon and hot when Skipper pedaled into the town that seemed on the map to be closest to Llangollen. There was one main street, with half a dozen parked cars and no pedestrians. Skipper rode the half-mile length of the street, past a grocery store, a drug store, a post office, a cafe that seemed to be closed, a car dealer's and a gas station, a barber shop. A young woman came out of the grocery store, gave him a curious glance and said, "Hey." He had learned along the way that "Hey" was the Carolina equivalent of "Hi." He said, "Hey," locked his bike and went into the store. He was hungry. It took him a minute to get used to the dark interior, and then he saw two long counters with stacked shelves behind them, and more piles of cracker boxes, cans of food, and a big wheel of cheese on one of the counters. He made his way around a washing soap display and past a Coke machine to the far end of the store where a man in a white apron watched him. Skipper felt uneasy.

The man said, in a voice neither friendly nor unfriendly. "Hey. What can I do for you?"

I should have gotten a haircut, Skipper thought. I probably look like a hippie. He glanced down at his dusty jeans and the sweat-stained T-shirt.

"Well, I thought I'd get a Coke. Kind of hot on the road." Skipper tried to laugh but his voice broke.

"Right behind you."

"Yeah. Sure. Thanks." He fumbled for the right change and dropped a quarter. It rolled under the counter and he had to get down on his hands and knees to find it. He wanted to flee, but this was ridiculous, intimidated by a country store, for gosh sake! He got up and put his coin in the slot and took out the cold bottle. The door opened and two young black boys came in. They gave him the same inquiring look the woman had given him.

He pried the cap off the Coke, looked the older boy in the eye and said, "Hey."

The boy said, "Hey, how you," and gave him a shy grin. Skipper felt better. The storekeeper greeted the boys by name, and they bought candy bars and left, glancing sidelong at Skipper. The younger one giggled.

Unexpectedly, when they had gone, the storekeeper said, "Them two is the Peterson boys. Good boys. You didn't need to have locked your bicycle."

Skipper was startled. The man must have been watching him before he came in. "I always lock it," he said. "Just a habit, I guess."

24

The man nodded. "We don't lock up much down here. You're a Yankee, I reckon." His manner was matter-of-fact.

"I guess that's what I am. Everybody seems to think so. I'm from Colorado."

"Oh." The voice was a little warmer. "Thought you might be from New York or somewheres up there."

"No. I've never been to New York." He picked up a box of saltines.

"Would you cut me about half a pound of cheese, please?" He pointed to a block of cheddar.

The storekeeper cut the cheese and wrapped it in a piece of waxed paper. Skipper paid him and as he walked away, the man said, "Just passin' through?"

Skipper began to feel annoyed. "I'm looking for some relatives."

"Kin? Hereabouts?"

Skipper ignored the question. "Can you tell me how to get to Llangollen?"

"Llangollen?" He looked blank.

"Well, I suppose they'll know at the post office." Skipper headed for the door.

"Hold on a minute. I can tell you." He came to the door and pointed south. "Down the road, take your first right. Go a mile till you come to one road and then a second that crosses yours. Go left, past the tennis court." His small eyes squinted, as if he were unaccustomed to sunlight. He watched Skipper unlock his bike. "You any kin to the Phillipses?"

Skipper straddled the bike and called back over his shoulder, "I *am* a Phillips." He rode away feeling he had scored a point.

Outside of town he stopped and ate the crackers and cheese, wishing he'd bought another Coke. He sprayed himself so thoroughly with Off, the smell made him slightly ill. There were mosquitoes, clouds of them, all right, and midges, and something else—yellow jackets—that buzzed him with apparent disregard for the Off. He picked a gardenia blossom, feeling a bit guilty, and put it behind his ear. "Olé!" he said aloud. But as he rode along, it occurred to him that the yellow jackets were attracted by the flower. Reluctantly he laid it in the coarse grass by the roadside. He wished his mother could see the flowers; they'd blow her mind. A bush covered with small white blossoms smelled as sweet as the gardenias, and there were bushes with lavender blossoms something like lilacs.

He made the turns the storekeeper had mentioned, and after a while he came to the tennis court, set back from the road and so well screened by bushes that he almost missed it. No one was there but it was well kept up. Jordan would have been interested, he had played in state championship matches before he got sick. He rested his bike against the metal gate and sat down on a bench. Now that he was so close to finding the Phillips family, he felt nervous. They might not want to see him. Obviously his father and the family weren't on good terms. Would they look at him and say "Yankee!" and turn up their noses? If they did, he'd get mad. His mother was from Michigan and her family were just as good as any old Tarheels, any day in the week.

He walked the bike down the narrow road, woods on his left, a wide grassy field on his right. A gum tree thrust roots into the path. He came unexpectedly upon a rambling house set in a grove of tall pines. The name on the mailbox was Phillips. He started up the path. Somewhere in the house a stereo was playing piano music. A concerto, Rachmaninoff, he thought. It stopped abruptly and the place was so quiet, he heard the scrape of the needle as someone lifted the tone arm. A careless way to treat a record. Near the front steps he stood still, not sure whether he ought to go up to the door or not. He had a funny feeling that he was intruding where he shouldn't.

Then he heard other sounds that he couldn't place. A metallic rasp and click, then a slammed door, and a crunching sound like the sound of his bike tires on dirt. He half turned to go, but just then a girl in a wheelchair came around the corner of the house. For a second she didn't see him, and he was startled by the look on her face: pain? rage? anguish? He wasn't sure what it was. Then she looked up and saw him. She stopped the wheelchair at once. She was beautiful, but her face was hostile.

"What do you want?"

"Well, I was just . . ." He couldn't get his words together. All he had to say was, "I'm looking for my father. George Phillips." But she scared him into silence, and for a moment they stared at each other.

She lifted a whistle that hung on a ribbon around her neck and blew it. The shrill sound terrified Skipper.

"Hey," he said, "I was just . . ." He heard hurrying footsteps from the back of the house.

"Gwyn, honey, I'm comin'. You all right?" It was a woman's voice, and he heard the sound of quick, heavy footsteps. She came panting around the house, a tall, broad, black woman. She stopped when she saw Skipper, and said, "Where'd that hippie come from?" She moved toward him, flapping her apron as if he were a hen. "Git! Scat!"

Skipper got. Trying to hold onto his dignity he walked hurriedly back to the road and mounted his bike. Unnerved, he rode the path to its end and followed another road, past

27

houses he didn't even glance at, until the road ended at a wide, black river. He splashed cool water over his face and hands and arms and sat down on an exposed cypress root, trying to calm down. He got out his canvas pack and put on a clean T-shirt and tried to brush the dust from his jeans. He had clean ones, but if he started to change his pants, that witch in the wheelchair and her bodyguard would be sure to swoop down on him and accuse him of indecent exposure. Probably boil him in oil, cut him up and sell the pieces for voodoo charms. He got his razor out of Alex's Dopp kit and cut his hair but he couldn't get it even. It looked as if he'd been run over by a mowing machine. He soaked his head in the river and combed his wet hair until it lay flat, the ragged ends hidden for the moment.

Sitting in a broken deck chair, he watched a lizard that lay motionless on a rock beside him. "What I should have done," he said to the lizard, "I should have worn a Brooks Brothers suit, see, and rented a Hertz car, and gone up to the door and presented my card. Mr. Rhys "Skipper" Phillips, Yankee, Boulder, Colorado 80302. Maybe they'd have let me in. But the heck with them. I'll go back to that town and ask the postmaster where I can find my father. He ought to know." On his way back he turned and looked at the river. It was a pretty river, wide and winding, with overhanging trees. He wished he could jump in and swim for about a mile. And not come back.

To avoid passing the house of the girl in the wheelchair, he took a different path that led him through woods. He passed a house set back among the trees, with a mailbox that read ANTHONY PHILLIPS. It was strange to see Tony's name spelled out on some stranger's mailbox in this faraway place. He began to be curious about these unknown relatives. He had never thought much about family, aside from his immediate family. Why, he wondered, were all these Phillipses living here? Did they own it? Llangollen sounded Welsh. Was he part Welsh?

After a moment of hesitation, he went up the path to the house of Anthony Phillips. The front door was open. He rang the bell, and a small dog appeared barking furiously and leaping up on the screen door. Skipper backed away.

"Hey, take it easy," he said. "I'm a member of the family."

The dog kept up its racket but no one came. "All right, all right," Skipper muttered. "So I look like a suspicious character. That seems to be the consensus. Skipper the Outcast." Through the trees outside the house next door he could see an oldish man with his back toward Skipper, filling a bird feeder. He must be deaf not to turn his head at all that racket. Was he Anthony Phillips? Skipper considered approaching him but lost his nerve. Maybe the man would bark at him too.

Instead, he went back down the road. Coming around a bend he saw another house, this one small and pretty with a lot of flowers. Day lilies bent their heads slightly in the breeze, and pansies bordered the walk. There were gardenia bushes along the front of the house, and at one corner a large magnolia tree leaned its shiny leaves over the roof. This time the mailbox said MARY RHYS PHILLIPS. That was getting close to home. His own name was Rhys Phillips. He stooped to empty the sand out of his shoe, and when he looked up again, a small elderly lady with white hair and bright blue eyes was peering at him. She had a trowel in her gloved hand, and for a second he thought. "Here we go again. She's going to attack." But instead she smiled and said in a soft voice, "Good mornin'. Lovely day."

Her sweetness was almost as unnerving to Skipper as hostility would have been. He wasn't prepared for it. He cleared his throat hoarsely and said, "Good morning. Yes, it is. Nice day, I mean." His voice broke. He pressed his hands to his head to smooth down his damp hair.

"I was just trying to decide where to put the azalea bush that Jim Charles gave me. Azaleas are not native to North Carolina, though that may surprise you because people always think they are. It needs sun but not blistering sun. I thought it might do well over here." She kicked with her small sandaled foot at a bare place near the steps. "Are you a gardener?" At his bewildered look, she gave a tinkly laugh and said, "I don't mean a *professional* gardener. I meant do you know about flowers?"

"Not very much," he said. "Mostly I just dig where my mother says dig, and weed where she says weed."

She laughed again. "She is fortunate to have a digger and weeder. My pesky arthritis slows me down."

He thought he had never heard such a soft, pretty voice, or such an enchanting southern accent. "I think I'm a relative of yours," he said impulsively. "My name is Rhys Phillips. People call me Skipper."

Her blue eyes widened, and she looked at him intently. "Goodness," she said. "Have I mislaid a cousin? Why don't I know you?"

"Well, I'm from Colorado."

She interrupted excitedly. "George! You're one of George Rhys's boys!"

"Yes, I am."

"But how lovely! Oh, do come in. Everyone will be so glad to see you." She led him into a cool, attractive living room with book-lined walls, pots and vases of flowers, and

30

a piano. She sat him down on a flowered chintz chair and said, "I'll bring you iced tea and then you must tell me all about yourself. I'll only be a minute."

Skipper grinned and sat back carefully in the chair, hoping he wasn't getting it dirty. This was more like it!

sixth

Skipper looked at himself in the round gilt-edged mirror of Mary Rhys's guest room. He had showered and changed to clean clothes and trimmed his hair more evenly with scissors he found in the bathroom. "You're no Robert Redford," he said to his image, "but you're in a state of cleanliness, and that's next to godliness." He saluted himself. "Carry on."

Mary Rhys was waiting for him, looking eager and tiny in a pale yellow linen dress. "I've been on the phone," she said. "I just had to tell Jim Charles and Mama-Maeve. This is Saturday, tonight we all eat dinner together in the Old House." She led the way to the road. "But first we call on Mama-Maeve and Papa-Rhys, your great-grandparents. You should know that your half brother, Gerald, lives with them."

So he had a half brother! That was news. Too much maybe, to absorb all at once.

"What is the Old House?"

"It's just a big old cabin really, the original house that George Rhys Phillips built when he came here from Wales in 1810. Squire Phillips, he was called. No one lives in the house now."

"Squire?" Skipper was impressed. "Is that like a lord or something?"

Mary Rhys laughed. "I'm afraid not. He was the biggest landowner in the Welsh village he came from. The gentry, you know."

Skipper didn't know. If he was descended from gentry, he'd have to find out what it was.

"I suspect we make too much of family," she said. "We're clannish." She waved to a black boy, about Skipper's age, who was chopping wood in a clearing. "That's Adam, one of Sally Maeve's children. Sally Maeve cooks for the school, and she and Lewie have looked after us for years. Before that, when I was a child, it was Sally Maeve's mother, Em. She's very old now. Sally Maeve and Lewie have ten children, and four of the five grown ones have gone to college. I think that's right fine, don't you? You'll meet Sally Maeve tonight at the Old House, she cooks our Saturday dinners during the summer. That's my Mama and Papa's house yonder. Papa is Anthony Phillips, your great-grandfather's brother. We live a long time. Oh, how I do chatter! But you're such a treat."

Skipper was trying hard to keep track. "Who are their children? Besides you, I mean."

"Jim Charles, he's the historian you were looking for. He's married to Savannah. Their children are Helena married to

Billy John Hayes, and Chick, married to Annie May. They come down summers from Raleigh. Chick's children are Jimmy, he's at Annapolis, and young Alex, he goes to The Citadel, and Savannah and Mary Gwyneth, both girls pretty as a picture, but Mary Gwyn had a terrible accident.

"Oh! Is she in a wheelchair?"

She looked at him quickly. "You saw her, did you?"

"Yes. I'm afraid I scared her. She thought I was a hippie."

"Oh dear. She's jumpy since the accident. She was such a promising pianist, you see, and now she feels helpless." She pointed to a partly visible chimney. "Yonder is Helena and Billy John Hayes's cottage. They've just come down for vacation, from Atlanta. They have two children. Bill John and Anthony."

"I'll never get 'em straight," Skipper said. "But I have a brother Anthony—"

"Do you indeed. Oh, I wish I knew you all. Who are the others?"

"My sister is Terry. She's married to a minister, and they have a baby, named Jordan after my brother who died." He went on quickly. "And besides Tony, I have a brother Alex."

"Oh." She was silent for a moment. "I had a brother Alex. He was killed in the war." She said it in a different voice, a quiet, preoccupied voice as if her thoughts had gone far back.

"Does a person ever—you know, ever get over it?" Skipper said.

She gave him a quick glance and touched his arm. "I suppose not really. But one learns to accept. The Lord makes us a loan of a beloved person, but there is no promise we can keep him forever." She directed him into a narrow path through woods. "Papa-Rhys and Mama-Maeve are very old.

34

Papa-Rhys had a stroke last year, and also he is quite deaf. I should perhaps tell you that Gerald is the apple of his eye. And I'm afraid he is bitter about your father. You may be a slight shock to him."

"Why is he so against my father?"

They had come in sight of the house. It was a one-story frame house to which a wing had been added. Bright annuals lined the walk, and a gardenia bush scented the air.

"We'll talk about it later."

A pretty young black girl with a dustcloth in her hand opened the screen door and smiled at Mary Rhys.

"Hey, Ellie May," Mary Rhys said. "You're home from college."

"Yes, ma'am."

"Ellie May goes to college over in Louisiana," Mary Rhys said.

Ellie May gave Skipper a quick smile.

"This is Skipper Phillips," Mary Rhys said. "Gerald's half brother."

Skipper saw the start of surprise and the change in Ellie May's expression, and wondered what it meant. This Gerald was going to be interesting to see.

He heard a patter of footsteps and in the cool dim hall a tiny lady appeared. She was old, but that was not his first impression. He was aware first of very bright eyes examining him with undisguised curiosity.

"Mama-Maeve," Mary Rhys said, "this is Rhys Phillips, George Rhys's boy, from way out in Colorado. He's called Skipper."

Mama-Maeve took one of Skipper's hands between her own small, veined hands. She gave a bright laugh, like a

35

girl's. "I am glad to hear that you are Skipper," she said. "We've got Rhyses aplenty around here. I'm right pleased to see you, child."

Skipper was delighted with her. "I'm glad to see *you*." And remembering southern manners, he added, "Ma'am."

She laughed again. "That's all right. Even our own young ones don't 'ma'am' and 'sir' us much anymore. How is your father?"

"I don't know. I came here to find him. I've never seen him."

"Oh." The old face with its tiny wrinkles looked shadowed for a moment. "We almost never see him, you know. He has the cabin that used to be slave quarters. He made it over for himself." She gave him a little smile. "Some kind of statement I believe he was making. Isn't that what they say nowadays? He comes down now and again, but he seldom comes near us." She changed her tone. "But where are my manners? Come in and sit down, you all. Ellie May will make us some of her good mint tea. I declare, I don't know how I manage when she's gone." She took them into a long, low-ceilinged room haphazardly but attractively furnished in a half-dozen styles and periods. Louvers at the windows made the room dim and cool, and for a moment Skipper didn't see the old man dozing in the big chair by the window.

Mama-Maeve walked across the room with her small, quick steps and put her hand on the man's shoulder. She bent toward his ear and spoke not loudly but slowly and distinctly. "Rhys, honey, there's someone to see us."

"Eh?"

"A young man to see us." She paused. "His name is Rhys Phillips."

The man gave her a startled look and turned his head slowly to bring Skipper into focus. He stared at him, one eye blinking rapidly, the other wide open. Skipper began to feel uncomfortable.

"How do you do, sir," he said.

The old man's pale eyes were fixed on him, and Skipper thought of that story about the Gorgon, whose face turned people to stone.

The old man looked at his wife, moving his head with difficulty. "Who?" he said.

There was a tiny pause before she answered. "George Rhys's boy. From out west."

Skipper saw the thin mouth twitch, and he wasn't sure whether it was the stroke or distaste for George Rhys's boy from out west.

He was a tall, thin man, this great-grandfather, with a thick shock of white hair, a white moustache, and pale blue eyes. His face was crisscrossed with deep lines. Skipper had never seen anyone so ancient. He looked for a resemblance. The profile perhaps was a little like Tony's, the long jaw and nose that Tony liked to call Roman. He wished this old man, his ancestor, would speak to him, or even look at him, but after that first cold stare, he had turned his face toward the window.

"Sit down and talk to us, dear," his great-grandmother said. "Mary Rhys, call to Ellie May and ask would she be an angel and bring us tea. Oh, here she comes. She always knows just what I want. Tell me about your mother."

They all talked so much and so fast and changed the subject with such bewildering speed. "My mother teaches at the university," he said.

"What department?" Mary Rhys asked. She got up and helped Ellie May with the tea things. Skipper started to help but she waved him back. "You're company. What does your mother teach?"

"English. Nineteenth century English poetry mostly, and the novelists, Dickens and Thackeray and that bunch. But some Shakespeare and that sort of thing, too."

"Mary Rhys is Chaucer," Mama-Maeve said. She laid her hand on Skipper's knee. "And you're not company, darlin', you're family."

Mary Rhys smiled and gave Mama-Maeve her tea. "Visiting family."

"I don't feel like family yet." Skipper said. And then afraid he'd sounded rude, he added. "I mean I never knew you existed."

"No, of course George Rhys wouldn't have told you."

Mary Rhys said, "Mama-Maeve, he's never even seen George Rhys."

"Yes, dear, so he said. Never seen his daddy. Nor granddaddy either. Your grandparents were killed, you know— our George Rhys, your daddy's daddy, and your grandmother."

"Yes, I did know that. In a car crash, wasn't it?"

She nodded. "May 2, 1934. Your daddy and Gwyneth were tiny children. We raised them." She glanced at her husband and then took the tea that Ellie May had for him. She raised her voice a little and touched his arm. "Tea, honey."

He took the cup and saucer in a hand that shook. Ellie May pulled a small table close to him, and he set the cup down with a clatter. "Thank you," he said in a low voice. Ellie May poured some cream into his cup, and he thanked her again.

"And now we're raising Gerald," Mama-Maeve said. She gave her little laugh. "We go on and on, parents forever."

"I'm anxious to meet him," Skipper said. "I didn't know I had another brother."

Mama-Maeve gave him a thoughtful look. "He'll be surprised. He's at a swim meet."

"Doesn't he know about us?"

"He's been told," Mary Rhys said, "but I expect it doesn't seem very real to him."

"I hope he wins his swim meet."

"Oh, he'll win," Mama-Maeve said. "Gerald always wins."

The old man spoke, startling Skipper. "Is Gerald back?" he said in a hoarse voice voice. "Is my boy back?"

Mama-Maeve spoke soothingly. "Not yet, honey. Not till 'round dinner time."

He subsided into silence again.

"We'll run along now, Mama-Maeve," Mary Rhys said, "and let you get your rest."

"Oh, pooh," Mama-Maeve said. "I never rest."

But Mary Rhys was on her feet. "I expect this boy could use a nap himself, riding all the way on his wheel."

Mama-Maeve gave him a mischievous smile. "Build up your strength for tonight, child. You'll see us altogether, and we're a formidable lot."

Skipper said goodbye to his great-grandfather, and the old man gave him a nod without looking at him. In the hall Mama-Maeve said, "Forgive him, dear. Your father hurt him so."

"But I'm not my father."

"No. But we don't think straight when we're hurt, you know." She reached up and kissed his cheek. "I'm so glad you've come."

39

He returned the kiss, feeling the papery skin of her face. "I like you."

She rested her head against his shoulder for a moment, and then straightened up and said to Mary Rhys, "Isn't he a love."

As they walked back toward Mary Rhys's house, a girl on a bicycle caught up with them. "Hey, Mary Rhys, wait up."

Skipper turned to look at her and instantly liked her. She was about eighteen, tall and long-legged, with reddish brown curly hair that came to her shoulders, and the same mischievous look that Mama-Maeve had, as if she enjoyed some private joke.

Straddling her bike she held out her hand. "Hey, cousin Skipper, I'm Savannah, daughter of Chick and Annie Mae, granddaughter of Jim Charles, sister of Mary Gwyn, Jim, and Alex, niece to Mary Rhys. You can't tell the players without a scorecard."

Skipper laughed. "What does that make you to me?"

"Faithful friend. Nearer than that. You'll have to get Mary Rhys to figure it out. She's the genealogist. Are you bringing him to dinner, Mary Rhys?"

"Yes, indeed."

"Oh, the poor lamb." She put her foot on the bike pedal. "Rest up, Skipper. We're an ordeal." She rode off in a small cloud of dust.

"Wow!" Skipper said.

Mary Rhys flicked dust from her eye. "Yes," she said, "you could say that."

40

seventh

As they came near the Old House, Skipper stopped in panic. The rambling log cabin seemed to be swarming with people.

"What is it?" Mary Rhys said.

"All that crowd! Are they all my relatives?"

She laughed. "I'm afraid so. Kin or folks who married into the family. Don't be shy. They're dyin' to meet you."

Skipper swallowed. "Well, here goes nothing." He followed her into the big room, and all conversation stopped as heads turned toward him. Holding him firmly by the arm, Mary Rhys said, "Everybody, this is Rhys Phillips, George's son from Colorado. He's called Skipper." She led him to the great-grandparents, who sat at one end of the room like royalty. "Mama-Maeve and Papa-Rhys, we're here."

41

Papa-Rhys inclined his head slightly, and his unblinking eye stared past Skipper.

"Good evening," Skipper said, feeling awkward.

"Bless you," Mama-Maeve said. "It's nice to have you here. Introduce him, Mary Rhys."

"I'll start right here and go by families. This is my brother Jim Charles, the historian you were looking for."

The tall, scholarly-looking man in glasses shook hands warmly. "Welcome to the clan, Skipper."

"And his wife, Savannah. That's their son Chick in the red sweater, and his wife Annie May. You met young Savannah." Savannah gave him a gay little wave and a wink. "Jim and Alex are off in a sailboat, Chesapeake Bay. And Mary Gwyn . . ." She paused a second. "Mary Gwyn didn't come?"

"She has a headache," her mother said quickly.

Because of me, Skipper thought, because of the wheelchair.

Mary Rhys introduced Helena and Billy John Hayes, and Skipper felt his second shock of hostility. Billy John, a stocky man with black hair and a mouth that turned down in perpetual scorn, said, "How you, cowboy," and managed to make it sound insulting.

Mary Rhys went on quickly, pointing out the rest of the family, old people, middle-aged people, children. Skipper knew he would never get them straight.

A tall slender woman with blue eyes said, "I'm your Aunt Gwyn and this is my husband Adam." She gave him a warm smile as he shook hands with her and his bald, pleasant-looking uncle. She gave him a warm smile, "Come on and meet Sally Maeve. She dotes on your daddy." She led him out of the crowded room, away from all the scrutinizing eyes, and as if she saw his relief, she said, "You can use a breather. That's too much family to put you through all at once."

42

He smiled gratefully. "I came looking for a father and I found at least a thousand relatives."

"Sometimes they seem like a million." She led the way through the long dining room to the kitchen. A plump black woman stood at the stove, picking up a piece of fried chicken with a pair of old silver tongs. The boy Skipper had seen in the field was carrying in stove wood, and a girl about his own age was counting out forks and knives.

"Sally Maeve, I've got a surprise for you," Aunt Gwyn said. "This is Skipper, George Rhys's youngest boy from out west."

Sally Maeve dropped the tongs and broke into a wide smile. "I declare!"

"Hello," Skipper said, feeling suddenly shy.

"Oh, don't he favor his daddy!" Sally Maeve said. "Right 'round the eyes." She slashed her apron toward her daughter and said, "Francie, you mind what you doin' there." Francie dropped a fork and giggled. "Got a mind like a flea, girls that age," Sally Maeve said. "Mr. Skipper, I'm purely proud to meet you. You got a good appetite on you like your daddy? That boy had the biggest appetite of any child I ever raised."

"My mother says I have." He liked the idea that this nice woman had "raised" his father. It must all connect with me somehow, he thought, but he wasn't sure yet what the connections were. He felt as if he had landed on a strange island where people spoke a language almost but not quite his own. "But if you call me *Mister* Skipper, I won't know who you mean."

Aunt Gwyneth and Sally Maeve looked at each other and laughed.

"Just habit, honey," Sally Maeve said.

43

"This boy's a westerner," Aunt Gwyneth said. "Out where they say, 'Smile when you call me that, Mister.' "

"Well, we'll just call him whatever he's a mind to be called." Sally Maeve's dark eyes looked him over with affection. "I sure am glad to see him. Maybe now we can get Mr. George Rhys down here."

"We're going to work on it," Aunt Gwyn said.

"That's what I came for," Skipper said.

" 'Course you did. Wasn't that nice, now, coming all that way. George Rhys is going to be tickled to death."

"It sure smells good in this kitchen." Skipper said.

She laughed. "You're just like your daddy." She followed Aunt Gwyn and him to the dining room door. "You eat up hearty now. No little pickin' bird."

Aunt Gwyn detained him a minute in the cool dining room, pointing out family group pictures taken over the years. He could read nothing in the pale blur of his father's face. "Am I like him?"

"You are a little, around the eyes." She studied one of the old pictures for a moment and sighed. "That was a long time ago. Look, there's Sally Maeve, slim as a willow then. I suppose we seem very antebellum to you, all the 'Miss' and 'Mister' business, and the family thing. I've noticed that the little habits fade away last." She pointed to a snapshot of a man with a beard. "That's Papa-Rhys in his salad days."

"He doesn't like me."

"It's not you. He set his face like a flint when George Rhys disappointed him so often. Don't take it personally." As they went to join the others, she added casually, "And your father's latest adventure hasn't helped. He's living with a black woman. She sounds fascinating, but Papa Rhys is not fascinated."

44

Before Skipper could think what to say, there was a stir in the room and people's faces turned toward the door. Someone was coming down the path, singing a happy-sounding song in a light tenor voice.

"It's Gerald!" The children rushed to the door, and the others watched expectantly—all except Savannah, who turned away and studied a picture on the wall as if she had never seen it before.

Mama-Maeve said in her husband's ear, "It's Gerald," and for the first time he smiled.

Skipper's stomach muscles tightened. The door was flung open and a tanned, handsome boy stood on the threshold, smiling. Skipper's head spun. He grabbed at a chair back. He thought he was going to faint. The boy in the doorway looked exactly like Jordan at thirteen. Jordan alive!

He felt Aunt Gwyn's hand on his arm. "Skipper, are you all right?"

"Yes. I . . ." He couldn't finish.

Gerald had gone at once to Papa-Rhys. Smiling down at him he said, "I won, Papa-Rhys. I'm county champion."

The voice was different. Lighter, somehow more sure of itself than Jordan's at that age. But the face, the face! He was taller than any of them had been at thirteen, but his build was like Jordan's—graceful, well-proportioned, broad-shouldered. He tossed his hair back from his forehead with Jordan's gesture. But the hair was brown and smooth, not Jordan's hair.

Papa-Rhys said in his hoarse voice, "Good boy, Gerald. I knew you could do it." He reached up a trembling hand and patted him.

Mama-Maeve said, "Gerald, there's someone here to meet you."

45

The boy turned toward her with easy courtesy. "Who?" He saw Skipper, and his smile was questioning.

"This is Rhys Phillips."

"Not another cousin!" He laughed.

"No, dear." Mama-Maeve watched his face. "He's your half brother."

Gerald stopped smiling, and he seemed to turn pale under his tan. Then he managed a little laugh. "That's a shock," he said. "A brother!"

"Hello," Skipper held out his hand and noticed it was trembling. Touching this boy, whose muscular hand was warm and alive, was almost too much for him. He tried to explain his emotion. "You shook me up, too. You look . . . you look so much like one of my brothers."

"How many of you are there?" Gerald said, in a polite voice, as if he were making conversation.

"Two other brothers and a sister."

Gerald looked at the others. "How about that. An instant family."

"Not exactly instant, dear," Mama-Maeve murmured.

"That western woman," Papa-Rhys said in an unexpectedly loud voice.

From the dining room a bell rang.

"Saved by the bell," Savannah said under her breath.

"Soup's on," Billy John said. "Shall we break up this touching reunion of long lost brothers and eat?" He poked Uncle Adam in the ribs. "You and me first, curly."

"Oh, do knock it off, Billy John," Savannah said sharply.

Her mother murmured something to her, and she said audibly, "But why does he have to put everybody down all the time?"

Skipper glanced back from Savannah to Gerald. He was smiling in some shared understanding at Billy John.

"Skipper," Mama-Maeve said, taking his arm, "you will please sit beside me." He moved to join her, wondering what the obvious alliance between Gerald and Billy John meant.

The long table was heaped with platters of fried chicken, bowls of blackeyed peas, yams, ears of corn, and hot corn bread. Gerald sat on his great-grandfather's right as if it were his accustomed place. Savannah's mother, Cousin Annie May, sat on Skipper's left, and Uncle Adam across from him. Still stunned by Gerald's striking resemblance to Jordan, Skipper kept looking at him, and it was hard for him to keep track of the family conversation that flowed around him, talk about when Herbert and Amy would be down, whether anything had been stolen from Herbie's cabin when it was broken into, whether Lewie ought to rotate from soybeans to something different. Skipper's head spun.

"You eat like a bird," Mama-Maeve said to him. "You won't find fried chicken like this when Sally Maeve's generation is gone."

"And *no* place in Yankee country," Billy John said, curling his lip slightly as if Yankee country were some unspeakable land. "When Sally Maeve and her lot are gone, we'll be eating on Colonel Sanders, just like you'all."

"The Lord forbid," Aunt Gwyn said.

Papa-Rhys made his first comment. "Ellie May's a good cook. She fed me fine when I was so poorly."

Mama-Maeve smiled and shook her head, and Aunt Gwyn said distinctly, leaning toward her grandfather, "Ellie May's not going to cook for folks, Papa Rhys. Ellie May's going to be a doctor."

He scowled, and his unmoving eye looked baleful. "Against nature," he said. "No good'll come of it."

Mama-Maeve turned quickly toward him, but she only said, "Now, Gerald honey, tell us about your next swimming meet."

eighth

JOURNAL: It's all very confusing. This horde of people, all related to me. But the thing that really throws me is Gerald, the half brother who looks just like you, Jordie. I thought I would really faint when I saw him. He's only thirteen, but he's as tall as I am, and very cool looking. Shape of the head, features, eyes, just like you, but his hair is light brown, and yours was red, his is straight and kind of flat to his head. I couldn't stop staring at him. His voice is different, but some of his facial expressions are yours—like the way you wrinkled up your nose when you were amused. His manner is different, he's very sure of himself, but that's because he's been spoiled, I think. Everybody seems to be charmed, except Savannah. I don't know why she doesn't like him; she doesn't seem like a jealous type, but I guess you don't really know people this quick. The young kids think he's Superman. They even open doors for him. Old Jordie, you never got that kind of treatment, did you. I don't know if you'd have liked it.

Cousin Annie May asked me to go see her daughter, Mary Gwyn, the one in the wheelchair, today. She told me about the accident: Mary Gwyn was a real super rider and she was thrown at a jump at some horse show. Injured her spine. She's had a lot of surgery but nothing has helped. What a horrible thing. I'm scared to go see her, partly because I can't believe she wants to see me or any stranger. (Who would?) But her mother wants me to "take her mind off her troubles."

There are so many Rhyses, Alexes, and Anthonys here, I almost feel at home. But they aren't the same, and there are no Terrys, no Jordans. You two were named for Mom's family. Funny how I never thought of family at all except the one underfoot. Funny how names and looks and characteristics go back and back. There are some oddballs. I really loathe Billy John Hayes, but he's only married into the family, he's not "one of us." (I'm catching on fast to the clan spirit.) I'm asked to stay awhile. Should I? Aunt Gwyn is sending for my father. Our father, I mean. (Do I call him Dad? Father? Pater? Pop? Papa-George-Rhys? Endless possibilities.) Oh, he must come. I've got this crazy idea that if I could get him to Colorado, even to visit . . . Well, we'll see. Tomorrow I'm going canoeing with Gerald. A chance to get acquainted, I hope, but my stomach turns over, really it does. I look at him, you know, and my breath stops, as if somebody stomped on my solar plexus, and then he smiles, and it's not your smile. Jordie, I don't know how to deal with it. I really don't.

50

ninth

The canoe ride with Gerald was interesting and strange. The river, dark and silent and fast-flowing in the center, twisted and turned and was full of unexpected rocks and half-exposed cypress knees. The branches of the trees hung low on both sides, filtering the sunlight into shifting patterns. Gerald insisted that Skipper ride as passenger—mostly, Skipper suspected, so Gerald could demonstrate his skill. And he *was* skilled. He guided the canoe unerringly past obstacles, into the current when he wanted to move fast, into shadowy coves to point out something to Skipper or just to paddle idly for a moment. Skipper sat facing him and listened attentively as Gerald talked. And Gerald did talk a great deal. Before an hour was up, Skipper knew that Gerald resented Savan-

51

nah, admired Billy John, counted heavily on his great-grandfather's support in all his activities. And Skipper heard at length about his swimming, tennis, debating, and other school triumphs. Skipper listened with amused tolerance to his new brother's self-confident account of himself. He could remember being pretty cocky himself at that age. When you were one of the younger ones, you had to crow good and loud.

Then in a sudden change of tone Gerald said, "How long you planning to stay?"

"Well, I don't know. Not long. I hadn't planned to stay at all when I first came. But everybody says wait and see if my father comes . . . I came to see him, you see. I wanted to ask him . . ." He didn't finish, but Gerald didn't notice. He simply seemed relieved, and said, "It's no use waiting for him. Even if he came, he wouldn't give you the time of day."

Skipper felt a need to defend his father. "My brother and I talked to him once on the phone. He asked us to come see him. He sounded nice."

"Nice!" Gerald spat into the river. "He's no good. He's a bum. Did you know he's living with a black woman?"

Skipper shrugged. "That's his business."

Gerald held his paddle still in midstroke, and the water dripped slowly from the blade. "Yankees!" he said, with disgust.

Skipper decided he had better change the subject. "What a neat river this is. You're lucky to live here."

Gerald began moving again, and for a few minutes the only sounds were the rhythmic cleaving of the water by the paddle, and the rat-a-tat-tat of a big woodpecker somewhere nearby.

Skipper broke the silence. "I'm going to meet Mary Gwyn today. I hope she won't mind."

Gerald shrugged. "She's shut herself up like a hermit."

52

"She wasn't always like that, was she?"

"Oh, no." He gave a little laugh. "She was the big athlete. Super horsewoman, great tennis player, promising pianist. But not any more . . . Papa-Rhys says pride goeth before a fall."

Skipper was startled. "Did he say that about Mary Gwyn?"

"No. It's one of his sayings."

Skipper was amused. Papa-Rhys the oracle, quoting the Bible or whatever, and Gerald thinking it was his own. "You're really fond of the old man, aren't you."

"Naturally. He's better than any father." Gerald steered the canoe into a cove where there was a sandy beach. "This is where we usually have picnics."

"It's great," Skipper said.

"They're all jealous of me," Gerald said. "You may have noticed."

"Because you win all the meets?"

"No, because I'm Papa-Rhys's favorite." He gave Skipper a long stare. "I'm the heir."

"I see." Skipper smiled. "Going to inherit the squireship. are you?"

"I'm serious. I inherit Llangollen."

"How do you mean?"

"The people here don't own their places. Papa Rhys owns the whole thing. He just leases to them." Gerald leaned forward and rested his elbows on his knees. The dark water lapped against the bank with a restful sound. "Billy John and I have got a few schemes up our sleeve about this land."

Skipper was startled. "Billy John!"

"Sure. Billy John's got good ideas. Money-making ideas."

"You don't mean you'd develop the place, do you? Sell to strangers?"

53

Gerald laughed. "For a Yankee that sounds funny. Llan-gollen will be finished when Papa-Rhys dies. He's all that holds it together."

"But at least you'd give the family first choice?"

Gerald shrugged. "If they can come up with the money." Then as if he realized he had been talking too freely, he said, "All that's a long way off. Don't say anything about it. Especially not to Mama-Maeve. It's not your headache anyway, all you'd stand a chance to lease would be the slave cabin." He laughed.

Bill John, Junior, came running down the path with a tennis racket. "Hey, Gerald, want to play?"

"Sure." Gerald headed the canoe into the beach. "You and who else?"

"Me and Phil will take you on, all right?"

"Be right with you." Remembering his manners he said to Skipper, "Do you mind?"

"Of course not. I've got some visits to make anyhow."

He helped Gerald beach the canoe and watched him run off with young Bill John. He shrugged. The kid was only thirteen, after all. Why shouldn't he show off a little? He had done it plenty himself. But Jordan never had.

tenth

Skipper ran his hands over his hair nervously. "Have I got ketchup on my chin or anything?"

Savannah laughed. "No, you're gorgeous. Just don't let Mary Gwyn know you put ketchup on barbecue. What Yankee barbarism!"

"That's me, Skipper the Barbarous." He stopped and looked at Mary Gwyn's house. "Well, into the battle." He made a sweeping gesture with his arm. "Shall we?"

"Relax. Gwynnie is a darling." She led him up the steps, knocked on the door, and opened it, calling, "Gwyn, are you ready for us?"

The black woman who had so alarmed Skipper when he first came appeared in the hall, all smiles. "Howdy, Savannah. Y'all come right in. Mary Gwyn'll be here in a minute. Glad to see you," she said to Skipper. "We didn't rightly know who you was the other day. We didn't mean to run you off like a stranger."

Skipper grinned. "Well, I was a stranger. I didn't even know I had a cousin living here."

"Ten thousand," Savannah said. "Poor Skipper. I'll go get Gwynnie, shall I?"

The woman looked apprehensive for a moment, but Savannah said, "It's all right, Mamie," and went into another room.

"She's a caution, that Savannah is," Mamie said. "Why don't you just set a minute, Skipper, and I'll see if they need help."

Skipper watched her go. Savannah had told him that she was not a local person, but a practical nurse whom Mary Gwyn had liked so much when she was in the hospital that she had persuaded her to come and live with her.

He looked around the small room. It was nice, white-walled, with framed English hunting prints and dark red curtains. One wall held books from floor to ceiling, and on the inside wall there was a small piano. The chairs were squashy and comfortable. But not for a paraplegic. He heard the faint squeak of wheels in another part of the house, and his stomach muscles tensed. How should he behave? Then he thought of Jordan hating it when anyone acted different because of his illness: the thing to do was to act natural. But how could you act natural while you were ignoring the most conspicuous thing about the other person?

He had no time to think about it. Savannah appeared in the doorway and said, "Come in and be presented."

56

Skipper jumped up and knocked a magazine to the floor. Awkwardly he replaced it and followed Savannah to a glassed-in porch where sunlight streamed in. The rattan furniture was covered with bright chintz. In a corner, her back to the light, sat Mary Gwyn in her wheelchair. She was wearing light blue slacks and a matching blue linen shirt. She looked like Aunt Gwyn, only with a more somber expression. Her face was pale, with dark circles under the eyes, and there was a look of strain.

She held out her hand while Savannah said, "Here he is, Gwynnie. Your latest cousin, the Yank from Colorado. Skipper, this is my sis, Mary Gwyn. In the cousin department you can't do any better."

Mary Gwyn's handshake was strong. "I apologize for being such an ogre the other day. I thought you were a stranger."

He smiled down at her, almost forgetting to be nervous. "I *was* a stranger."

"Anyway, it's 'ogress,' " Savannah said. "Look, you guys, I've got to run. I'm playing tennis . . ." For just a second she hesitated, as if she wished she had not said that. ". . . with Ernie Jacoby, and he's a demon. He never lets me win."

Gwyn said, "Go ahead, and beat the pants off Ernie Jacoby. Quote—you can do it if you try—unquote." She gave Savannah a wry smile. "Sound familiar?"

Savannah bent down and kissed her sister lightly on the forehead. "Have a good time with Skipper. He's kind of scared of us." And she left.

Skipper sat down, and the two looked at each other for a moment in silence. Then Mary Gwyn said, *"Are* you scared of us?"

He started to say no, but instead he said, "Of course, I am."

"And of me especially, because you don't know how to treat me. 'Shall I pretend she's running around on two legs?' you wondered. 'Or shall I offer sympathy and clichés? Hope on a platter, along with iced tea?' " She made a slight gesture toward him with one hand. "Now I really am being embarrassing. Pay no attention."

"Well, I'm not embarrassed," Skipper said, and it surprised him to realize he was not. "I thought I would be, but I have a funny feeling as if I've known you a long time."

For a moment she didn't answer. She was looking down at her hands and when she looked up again, her eyes were bright, as if tears threatened. But she laughed. "Usually people act as if I've died and they're trying not to notice."

"Maybe it's different for me because I didn't know you before," Skipper said. "Or maybe it's Jordan that makes the difference. My brother."

"The one that died of amyotrophic lateral sclerosis."

"You know about him?"

"Savannah told me." She changed her tone. "Well, how about a glass of sherry? Are you too young?"

He grinned. "I guess a sip or two won't send me down the road to hell."

She called to Mamie. "Mamie, why don't you bring in the Tio Pepe and three glasses. We'll toast our new boy."

"Sure thing, honey." Mamie reappeared in a few minutes with the chilled bottle and glasses and a plate of crackers.

Mary Gwyn lifted her glass toward Skipper. "Here's to Skipper."

She talked a good deal, in her own abrupt way, quizzing

58

him about his reactions to Llangollen, and never referring to herself again. She looked a little like her sister Savannah, but the face was stronger, the jut of the chin almost defiant, and her manner of speaking more positive than Savannah's good-natured drawl. Except for Gerald, she was the best-looking of his new relatives.

When he said something about the pleasures of finding the Phillips family, she gave her short laugh and said, "But don't you find it a bit odd?"

"Odd?"

"The family huddling together in this little corner of the world, the squire and his entourage in a fortified castle."

"It *is* unusual."

"We're like a family marooned on a far planet with no way back." She stirred restlessly and then in a different tone began to chat about his family, asking questions about his sister and brothers.

He found he was glad to talk about them; it made them seem a little closer. The familiar in the middle of the unfamiliar.

Finally she said, "Well, Skipper, it's my nap time."

He jumped up in remorse. "I'm sorry. I've stayed too long."

"Not a bit. I enjoyed it." She gave him a wry smile. "And you're not used to people who have to take an afternoon nap."

"Oh, but I am. I carried my brother upstairs for a rest plenty of times."

She looked down at her hands for a moment. "Did he mind?"

"Sure he minded."

She gave him a quiet look and then said, "Will you wheel me into the living room? It will save calling Mamie back. She gets tired."

He wheeled her into the room where the piano was and lifted her onto the couch."

"You'd make a good nurse." She gave him her half-defiant little smile that said, "Don't pity me."

"Like I said, I've had practice."

"Come back again, will you? I'd like to hear about Jordan."

"I'll come."

He walked slowly down the road to the river. Mary Gwyn had stirred up memories. Lifting her like that, he had almost felt as if he had Jordan in his arms. Her look of pain and defiance and fear was familiar to him. Jordan had suffered and hated it and been frightened, no matter how brave the front he had put up. It seemed to Skipper that he understood all that about Jordan better now than he had at the time. Then his own feelings had been too mixed-up with his observations. He stopped and sat down on a fence post. It was surprising how the sky seemed to come right down like a blue tent, with no break in the flat land to distort it. It was natural that people looked at the sky when they thought of heaven; where else *could* you look?

"Oh, Jordie," he said aloud, "it's such a beautiful day." He got up in a minute and walked on. What good was a beautiful day if you couldn't share it?

eleventh

Monday was a good day. Skipper played four sets of doubles with Gerald, Phil, and young Adam, and Gerald and Adam won three of the sets. He had discovered that Gerald was not a good loser. And although he wouldn't let himself throw a game just to see that radiant smile, he was relieved when Gerald came out ahead.

In the afternoon Skipper spent an hour with Mama-Maeve, the two of them alone in her sunny little sewing room, chatting comfortably about many things: The Rockies, which she had never seen, the changes in behavior among the generations, her interest in Sally Maeve's family, her old home in Ireland. "I'm the maverick, you know," she said, "the spanner in the Phillips works. I was born in Letterfrack, Connemara, County Galway, a thousand light-years from Wales and North Carolina."

He grinned at her. "I think the family needed a touch of Irish."

Her old face broke into tiny wrinkles of amusement. "I knew the minute I laid eyes on you, you'd got some of my Irish in you somewhere. It's that wicked glint in your eye. You're the one that makes them laugh at home, aren't you now?"

"They laugh *at* me mostly."

"It's good to make people laugh. The Phillipses can be so serious." She gave a little sigh. "Though they do sing like angels. You must come to our little chapel next Sunday and listen to them." She fluttered her hands. "Myself, I can't carry a note."

"Me, either," Skipper said.

"You're my boy. You're the Irish one." She leaned her head against the soft, faded blue velvet upholstery of her rocking chair.

He wanted to ask her if she thought George Rhys would consider coming to Colorado, but she seemed suddenly tired. He got up. "May I come back tomorrow?"

"Not only may but must."

He made a deep bow. "Majesty, your subject will attend."

She was chuckling as he went out the door. He stopped abruptly, closing the door behind him. Gerald was in the hall, and when he saw Skipper, he made a great business of hunting in the closet for a tennis racket. "Oh, hey," he said, as if caught by surprise, "I was wondering where you were. You want to go for a canoe ride?"

"The picnic is this afternoon."

"Plenty of time. Come on. I want to show you the new

public beach. Papa-Rhys loaned it to the village so anybody can come swim."

"That was nice," Skipper said.

Gerald grinned. "It's a good place to run into water moccasins." He was wearing bright blue swim trunks and a tank shirt, and he looked to Skipper like some kind of bronzed god.

"You're kidding," he said.

Gerald laughed. "Both human and reptile. Come on, I'm supposed to police the area and it's boring to do it alone."

Except for two small boys swimming in the river, there was no one at the little beach. Someone, and Skipper suspected it was Mama-Maeve, had arranged for two redwood picnic tables and benches and a pair of double hibachis that already showed signs of use. Skipper helped Gerald gather up discarded beer cans and pop bottles, dumping them in the new plastic trash can.

When they had finished cleaning up, Skipper washed his hands in the cool river water and watched his cousin dive in and swim to the opposite bank and back. He wished he had worn his own swim trunks: the air was sultry and still, and he was hot from the mild exertion. But he had dressed for the picnic in clean jeans and his only clean shirt, which Mary Rhys had laundered. He sat on a wooden stool watching Gerald's clean, smooth stroke, half listening to the sleepy sounds of birds and insects. The big trees hung brooding over the dark water. A mosquito bit him on the neck and he swatted it. He looked at his watch and called to Gerald, "It's almost time for the picnic."

Gerald turned lazily on his back and said, "No big deal."

Skipper began after a few minutes to feel nervous. They were going to be late for the picnic, and he hated to be late,

63

especially this time when Aunt Gwyn had arranged it for him. "Hey, Gerald," he called, "can I walk back from here?"

Gerald swam toward him and stood up, water showering off his shoulders and head, like a young Neptune. "What an antsy guy you are. Hold on a minute." He pulled a towel from under the bow seat in the canoe and dried himself off. "Nothing'll start till we get there."

Skipper had the uneasy notion that Gerald meant "I," not "we," but he dismissed it from his mind. It was just Gerald's cocky way of talking. They were in the canoe and ready to leave when Aunt Gwyn's young son Adam came running down the path, zigzagging and making sounds that faintly resembled an airplane engine.

"Gerald," he called, "wait up." He put on a burst of speed and made a perfect three-point landing on the edge of the river.

"What's up, if anything?" Gerald asked him.

"Mama says hurry up, they're waiting on you at the picnic, and BIG NEWS!" He paused importantly.

"Such as?"

"Mama talked to Uncle George Rhys on the phone. He's coming down." He ran off, revving his engines.

Skipper felt his heart jump. He was so moved by Adam's announcement that it was several minutes before he realized that Gerald, behind him in the stern seat, was absolutely still.

He turned to look at him and was startled by Gerald's expression of rage, so tightly controlled that the effort darkened his face. "What is it?" he said quickly. "You won't have to see him if you don't want to, will you?"

Gerald's paddle cut the water with such force that the canoe slewed around. Automatically Skipper put his own paddle in the water to straighten their course.

"I suppose he's only coming to look me over. That's what I'm here for," he said. "He won't bother you, will he?"

In a tight, almost trembling voice Gerald said, "He'll try to weasel in again. He knows Mama-Maeve's on his side. Now he'll have you to back him up."

"Back him up in what?"

"He hates me. He'd like to get me out of here. 'The Crown Prince of Llangollen,' that's what he calls me." Gerald sounded as if he were going to cry. "And what if he brings *her?* I'll be the laughingstock of the town. But he'd enjoy that."

"Oh, come on," Skipper said gently. "Of course, he doesn't hate you. I'll admit he'll never get any Father of the Year awards, but from what I hear, he's just kind of irresponsible, happy-go-lucky. Maybe he never really grew up."

Gerald didn't answer, but the strength of his paddling was sending the canoe up the river at alarming speed. They grazed a large cypress knee and seemed any number of times to be heading straight for a boulder, although Gerald's skill always avoided them.

"Take it easy," Skipper said, trying to sound as if he were joking, but Gerald's attitude irritated him. "I don't want to end up in the river in my only clean shirt."

"He'll cozy up to Mama-Maeve," Gerald said. "That's his game. He writes to her, you know, and calls her up. He knows she can influence Papa-Rhys."

Trying to sound reasonable Skipper said, "If he was into that kind of thing, he'd hang around more, wouldn't he, and try to please Papa-Rhys, not make him mad—"

"He hates my guts," Gerald said. "He deserted me."

They had come in sight of the picnic group. Savannah turned and waved. Mama-Maeve sat in a canvas deck chair, fanning herself with a bamboo fan. Aunt Gwyn was anchoring a paper tablecloth on the picnic table, and Uncle Adam was bending over the charcoal fire. Some of the children played with a beach ball.

"Cheer up," Skipper said. "I doubt if he's even given you a thought."

He had hardly finished speaking when the canoe veered sharply and overturned. Skipper floundered to the surface, choking a little from the unexpected dousing, and very angry. Gerald was behind him, treading water and trying to right the canoe. He was grinning.

Skipper stood up in waist-high water and looked back at his half brother. In a low, furious voice, he said, "Damn you, you did that on purpose."

"Don't be a bad sport, Skipper," Gerald said smugly. "It was an accident. I hit a snag."

"Snag, my eye." Skipper waded ashore, river water dripping from his shirt and jeans, and his tennis shoes squishing. The children were laughing, and Uncle Adam had turned around in surprise. Aunt Gwyn said, "Adam, run back to the house and get a dry T-shirt and those tan shorts of your father's. They ought to fit Skipper."

"I'm all right," Skipper said grimly. He was wringing the water out of his jeans.

"We can't have you catching your death, not at your own picnic. Here comes Mary Rhys with the chicken salad . . ."

Young Adam ran off on his errand, and Savannah led Skipper toward the fire. No one said anything to Gerald, who had beached the canoe and was rubbing himself down.

"What a stupid thing for me to do," Gerald said smoothly. "I know that snag is there, but I clean forgot it."

Uncle Adam glanced at him, but no one spoke. Mama-

Maeve was looking steadily at Gerald with an expression of sadness. Then she met Skipper's eyes and held his gaze for a moment. She shook herself a little, slapped at a gnat with her fan, and said briskly, "Now then, did anyone think to bring the sherry?"

twelfth

Mary Rhys stood on tiptoe reaching for a book on one of her shelves. "I have something here I thought your mother might like . . ."

"Let me get it," Skipper said.

"It's an old copy of 'The Rime of the Ancient Mariner.' Not old enough to make a fortune, I'm afraid." She blew dust from the gold-bordered leaves. "But old enough to intrigue her. I found it in a secondhand bookshop when I was staying at Alfoxden. I thought it was a good omen." She turned and smiled at him. "Alfoxden is the house where William and Dorothy Wordsworth stayed when they visited Coleridge. It's a small inn now, and I stood in my bedroom window and thought how Wordsworth must have looked out that same

68

window onto those same woods and fields, listened to those same early morning birds . . . Well, not the same birds of course . . ." She gave him a close look. "You're worrying about meeting your father."

"Does it show?" He tried to relax, feeling strained and uneasy after a mostly sleepless night. "Yes, I'm pretty nervous, to tell you the truth. I mean I've never had any experience in meeting fathers, my own, I mean. I'm not making any sense."

She patted his hand. "Perfectly natural. But what you need is your lunch now. I've made some chicken salad sandwiches, if you can face chicken salad again after the picnic."

He managed to smile. "I can face your chicken salad any time."

While they were eating lunch, he said, "You don't think Gerald will make a scene or anything, do you? He seemed so upset."

She didn't answer for a moment. "I think he will just stay away until your father has gone again."

They were finishing the Boston cream pie she had made and talking about snakes. In answer to his question she said, "Yes, there are cottonmouths and such. But they don't really bother people, if we don't bother them. They swim down the middle of the river minding their own business, and one keeps well out of the way. There's a tradition, if someone further upstream sees one, he calls out, 'Snake!' and the person at the next clearing hears him and calls, 'Snake!' It's a kind of warning system, you see."

A moment later Skipper looked out the window and said, "Snake!" Then he added quickly, "I was only joking . . ."

Mary Rhys followed his gaze and said, "Oh, yes. Billy John is coming to call on me. That's rather unusual."

"Listen," Skipper said, "I apologize. I didn't mean to—"

Quietly she cut him off. "No need to apologize. Billy John is not a family favorite."

"Except with Gerald."

She pulled her eyebrows together in a worried little frown. "One hopes Gerald will outgrow that influence. Billy John's values are not the same as ours. But one can't expect everyone . . ." She stopped and put down her napkin as the front door slammed.

"Why, Billy John, good afternoon," she said. "I'm so sorry I didn't hear you knock."

Billy John was in a state. His thick hair was rumpled and his face was flushed.

"I didn't knock, Mary Rhys," he said. "I'm not in the mood for peccadillos."

Peccadillos, Skipper thought, with a certain grudging admiration. That's a pretty good word to come up with when you're all riled up.

"You seem upset," Mary Rhys said. "Can I help?" Her voice was as polite and sweet as it always was, but there was a coolness in it too that Skipper had not heard before. I would not want to tangle with Mary Rhys on anything serious, he thought.

The tone obviously had its effect on Billy John as well. He spoke more calmly, but his face was still agitated. "Helena and I were in Raleigh yesterday, as you no doubt know."

"Yes. We missed you at the picnic."

"She had to go to that doctor . . ."

"I hope the news was encouraging."

He shrugged irritatedly as if the news of Helena's health was beside the point. "Same old malarkey. Just a waste of money in my opinion. Anyway . . ." His scowl deepened. "I didn't hear till just now that we're about to have a visitor. A very unwelcome visitor." He turned and glared at Skipper. "Gerald says your father is coming."

Skipper made a great effort to emulate Mary Rhys's control. "Yes, he's coming to see me. That's what I came for, to see my father."

"I don't give a hoot in hell what you came for. I don't want that bum moving in just a stone's throw from my house. What if he brings that nigger woman?"

Skipper felt the blood rush to his face, and he stood up. Mary Rhys touched his arm, and it was she who spoke. There was no trace of a smile now in her voice. It was cold as steel. "That's enough, Billy John."

"I suppose you condone him shacking up with that black harlot."

"I would not presume to tell him how to live his life, and you don't understand, Billy John, that no one in his family would ever refer to a friend of George's in that vulgar, cruel way. But you have never understood us—"

He interrupted, his voice rising. "Oh, I understand you all right. All sweetness and light, you Phillipses. I believe in straight talk. And I say George Rhys is no good, and I don't want him within a country mile of my kids."

Skipper stepped forward until he stood close to Billy John. "Mr. Hayes," he said, "I can't let you talk that way."

"*You* can't let me! Who do you think you are, a stupid kid, barging in here, total stranger, making trouble . . ."

"I don't know about any trouble I've made. My father is coming to his own house, to meet me. I can't see that it's any concern of yours."

Billy John thrust his face toward Skipper. "And I 'spose you can't wait to meet his friend."

"I'd like to meet her. She might turn out to be my stepmother. I'd like very much to meet her."

Billy John looked as if he might explode. He stood glaring at Skipper, fists clenched.

"Yankees!" He spat out the word and stalked out of the house.

Mary Rhys gave a little jump as the screen door slammed. "Poor Billy John," she said.

"Poor Billy John!"

"There's a cruelty in him, an insensitivity, that you feel comes from ignorance rather than evil. But ignorance is a kind of evil, isn't it." She broke off and looked up at Skipper. "You behaved quite splendidly just now."

Skipper was pleased, but he said, "I didn't do anything."

"That's just it. There is a time for holding one's tongue and a time for speaking out, a time for glaring and a time for a punch in the nose." She gave a delighted laugh. "Good heavens, what am I saying. You'll think I'm a savage."

"I think you're terrific," Skipper said.

But he went for a walk after he had helped Mary Rhys with the dishes because he was still angry and needed to walk it off. Billy John by himself was bad enough, but it worried him that the man had so much influence on Gerald.

As he walked past Papa-Rhys's house, Ellie May came running out. "You're wanted on the phone," she said.

The family! he thought, and ran for the house. Just so nothing was wrong . . .

Mama-Maeve was holding the phone in her hand, and she handed it to him. "It's your father, dear," she said.

72

"Oh!" That was the last thing he had expected. For a second he hesitated, rearranging his thoughts. "Hello? This is Skipper."

He remembered the voice, although this time his father sounded more sure of himself.

"Skipper? Good to hear your voice. How're you doin'?"

"Just fine," Skipper said.

"Good, good. Nice you could come—dig into the family roots and all that." He laughed. "That Mama-Maeve, she's something else, isn't she?"

"She's great." Skipper looked up, but Mama-Meave had tactfully gone into the living room. "They're all great."

"Well . . ." he drawled the word out. "I can't get *that* carried away. But I do like my sis. Old Gwyneth is a rare lady."

"Yes, she is." Skipper began to wonder if they were going to go through the whole family. "I'm awful glad you're coming down. I . . ." He almost gave up in a wave of shyness.

His father's voice changed slightly. "Well, old man, that's what I called about." Pause. "I'm awfully afraid I'm not going to be able to make it."

"You aren't coming?" Skipper couldn't keep the dismay out of his voice.

"Something's come up. Miranda, the lady I'm living with, had made plans for us that I didn't know about. I can't disappoint her."

"Oh, I see." Skipper waited a moment, but his father said nothing more. "I was hoping she'd come too. I'd like to meet her."

"Miranda? Come to Llangollen? Skipper, I'm afraid you're not very well clued in there yet. Miranda is a black woman."

73

"I know. So what?"

He sounded suddenly more friendly. "Well, in places like Colorado, so nothing. But Llangollen is a different story."

"I know that." Skipper thought of Billy John. "But only a few people would object . . ."

"One person objecting is more than I am about to put Miranda through. Anyway I'm proud you feel that way. Listen, we must get in touch. When are you going back?"

Skipper longed to say, "I came to see you!" But all he said was, "I'm not sure, but sometime soon."

"Well, I'll do my darndest to get down to see you. I do want to see you."

"I could come up there . . ." Skipper said tentatively, but his father either didn't hear him or didn't respond. "I have pictures of the rest of the family you might like to see . . ." He hesitated. "And of Jordan."

"Yes," his father said. "I always regretted . . ." But he didn't finish the sentence. In a heartier voice he said, "Listen, boy, we'll make it before you go, come hell or high water. Think positive. All right? We'll be in touch. I do want to see you, you know."

Skipper put the phone back on the hook. Maybe you do, he thought, but not as much as I want to see you. He looked up and saw Gerald on the stairs and wondered how long he had been there.

"Did he let you down?" Gerald said, coming down into the hall. "Did our dear father give you the shaft?"

"Of course not," Skipper said. "He just can't make it this time. He'll be down later."

"Don't count on it." Gerald went out of the house whistling.

thirteen

Skipper went to the river early for a swim. The sun was already hot, and the cool water and the soft black ooze that squished around his feet felt good. He flipped over on his back and floated in the easy motion of the inlet. Three young black children came down after a while, looked at him with mild curiosity, and splashed around knee-deep, shrieking, "It's cold! It's cold!" They ran out again and played ball with a pine cone and finally wandered away.

Skipper swam across the river and pulled himself up on the other bank, lying flat in the sun. He wished he knew whether his father would ever come, or whether he was stalling. It was hard to understand why he should hesitate because of his friend Miranda. Nobody but Billy John would make any fuss, and he needn't see Billy John. Maybe I should go up there and see him, Skipper thought; his father hadn't seemed very turned-on by that idea, but maybe he was shy. How peculiar not to know whether your father was shy or not. Tony might remember him enough to know those things.

Two Indian boys came down to get a canoe, one of them tugging a two-year-old by the hand. The little boy reminded Skipper of young Jordan, scuttling along like a small crab, and he felt suddenly desolated with homesickness. It was ridiculous hanging around here. Gerald resented him, Papa-Rhys couldn't stand him, and his father didn't seem all churned up to see him, so what was he doing here? It was time he got on with things. He'd call the airline about a reservation and then call his mother. He could ride the bike to Raleigh and catch a plane out of there. It was stupid to have come.

And yet he was glad he had gotten to know Mama-Maeve, Aunt Gwyn, and Mary Rhys, Savannah, Mary Gwyn. He'd been back to talk to her a couple of times; she was special. And in spite of Gerald's dislike of him, he was very glad he had met him. It was good to see where his father's family had come from. Llangollen was a nice place. It would be a shame if Gerald sold it off and it turned into another chintzy devellopment. But it might be years before Gerald could do that, and lots of things could happen in the meantime.

When he swam back and came out of the river, Gerald and Billy John were coming down the path, Gerald stooping now and then to pick up an empty beer can or Coke bottle or candy wrapper. Billy John was talking earnestly, and at first they didn't see Skipper. When they did, they stopped almost guiltily, as if they had been discussing him. Then they

76

came forward again, Billy John smiling his sour little smile.

"Well, well, speak of the devil," he said. "We were just talking about you, Skipper."

"Really?"

"Yeah, weren't we, Gerry. Heard you were leaving us soon."

"Then you must have a news source I don't know about. I don't know when I'm leaving."

"Oh? We heard you were leaving 'cause your daddy refused to come down and see you. Seems like a shame, doesn't it, a man refusing to come see his own boy that he's never laid eyes on. Never did see you, I understand, even when you were a baby." He shook his head. "Can't imagine treating my young Billy John that way, or any of my kids." He looked at Gerald. "But some daddies are downright unnatural."

"You can say that again." Gerald looked glum.

Skipper's good sense told him to walk away, but he was too angry. "Billy John," he said, "I have just about had it with your cracks about my father. I don't know what you've got against him but—"

Gerald broke in, in a furious tone. "I'll tell you what. He's plotting to get hold of Llangollen. Why else would he have got you here? You're supposed to weasel your way in with Papa-Rhys, so he'll put you in the will, and then George Rhys will have it all his way."

Skipper stared at him with his mouth open. "Are you out of your mind? My father didn't even know I was coming. He hardly remembered I existed."

"Oh, sure," Gerald said.

"Well, if that's the big plot, why isn't he down here to see me?"

77

"Because it's tricky. *He's* tricky. He's making it look as if he doesn't care anything about you, but all the time he's laying his plot."

Skipper looked at Billy John. "I suppose you're the one that dreamed up this fairy tale. I wouldn't have thought you had that much imagination."

To Skipper's surprise the remark hit home. Billy John flushed an angry red. "Got barnyard manners just like your daddy," he snapped, "insulting folks. Well, let me tell you, and you can tell him, your rotten little scheme won't work. Gerald here's got the inside track, and he's going to keep it. Your no-good pa, and you either, aren't going to make one jot or tittle of difference."

Skipper stepped up to Billy John and grabbed the front of his shirt. "You get out of here with your filthy mouth, before I get really mad and bust you to pieces."

Billy John, who was broader but shorter than Skipper, took a step backward, his eyes widening. "You'd better not lay a hand on me. Sometimes you push folks too far and they lose their self-control and do things you might not like."

"Are you threatening me, Billy John? I thought only poor white trash went around threatening people like that."

Billy John's face turned purple. "Are you calling me white trash?"

Skipper let go of his shirt. "If the name fits, you're welcome to it."

For a moment Billy John seemed about to fight. Then he turned and stalked off up the path.

Gerald spoke in a low voice. "If you know what's good for you, you better leave this place." He hurried after Billy John.

Skipper found himself shaking. Rage was not a comfortable emotion. He walked back to Mary Rhys's house, thinking about the scene that had just taken place. The "plot" Gerald had spoken of seemed so obviously absurd, it was hard to take it seriously, but Gerald seemed to believe it. Probably Billy John did too; it was the kind of thing he would go in for himself.

He didn't report the encounter to Mary Rhys, but in the evening he rode his bike into town and called his father from a pay phone. He told him what had occurred.

"I wouldn't bother you with it, only they seem to be taking it so big. I guess the best way to stop it is for me to clear out."

He had been afraid his father would laugh at him for taking it seriously, but he did not. "Billy John is always half a yard away from bankruptcy," he said. "I suppose he figures on getting himself appointed Gerald's guardian if anything happens to Papa-Rhys. Or *when* it does; it can't be far off. Then he'll fiddle and maneuver till he has his hot little hands on the land. Look, I'll really try to make it down there this weekend and have a talk with Mama-Maeve and my sister. It ought to be possible to put a checkrein on Billy John. Maybe Helena should be told, although she's not much use. Anyway, you stick around a little longer, okay?"

Skipper was glad he had called his father. It was a more satisfactory talk than he had expected. So he would hang on until the weekend. His father ought to know how to get things straightened out; he knew the family, after all.

Skipper bought a bottle of Coke, not dropping his money this time, and had a brief chat with the storekeeper. He bought a box of candy for Mary Rhys and rode home in the half-darkness, enjoying the flower smells and the soft sounds of evening. He felt more at ease than he had in some time.

fourteenth

Skipper walked over to Mary Gwyn's house, feeling the need of someone to talk to. When he came up the back path, he found Mamie picking pansies and stopped to speak to her, then turned in surprise at the sound of piano music from the house.

"She's doing a little playing," Mamie said.

"Should I go away?"

"No, don't go. You're good for her."

They both winced as Gwyn hit a wrong chord.

"Don't sound much like old times," Mamie said. "I heard her play over to the college before she was hurt." She rubbed at a spot of mud on her hand. "I asked to nurse her when I heard about the accident." Then in a more cheerful tone, she said, "You go along in and have a chair in the kitchen, and when she quits playing, you go on in. She won't play long. Upsets her too much."

Skipper went into the kitchen. Gwyn was playing something Skipper didn't recognize, and he wondered if she were improvising. Then she broke off and began again with the Grieg Sonata in A Minor. They had the record at home. It was strange to hear it played this way, without the pedals.

He closed his eyes and saw himself at home, up in the room that he and Jordan had shared, listening to the music, half listening for the old Volvo that would be his mother driving home from campus, half expecting Terry and the baby to stop by, or Tony or Alex.

The music broke off with a dissonant crash, and he sat still for a minute, staring into space. He got up when he heard the squeak of the wheelchair tires on the floor. Mamie came into the kitchen with her arms full of flowers. "Go in and see her," she said.

Reluctantly, afraid of upsetting her, he knocked on the door lintel. "Mary Gwyn? It's Skipper." He heard the chair swing away from the piano.

After a moment she called out, "Come in, Skipper. How nice." She was smiling as if nothing disturbing had happened.

"Is it all right? If you're tired, I could come back."

"Not at all. Please stay." She looked at him. "Is anything the matter?"

"Oh, I just had a bunch of stuff on my mind, and you're the one I come to."

"I'm flattered. Tell me all about it."

He told her about the scene with Billy John and Gerald.

She listened, and for a moment she was silent. "Skipper," she said at last, "why don't you go home?"

81

He was startled. "Go home?"

"I don't mean that the way it sounds. I mean Llangollen doesn't comfort you, it upsets you. Why get involved with Gerald and that odious Billy John and all that if you don't have to?"

"Gerald's my brother."

"But you never knew he existed. Go back to thinking you have only your Colorado brothers. Gerald, my dear, is a problem, but not yours."

"I keep feeling I ought to help. My big brothers always helped me."

"But that's different. Gerald only resents you. I don't mean to be cruel, but he sees you as a threat. He tends to see all of us as a threat, I think. And Billy John encourages it."

Skipper thought for a few minutes. "Well, I'll wait till my father comes down. He's coming this weekend. Maybe he'll be able to think of a solution."

She made an impatient gesture. "Skipper *darlin'*, George Rhys never solved a problem in his life. He creates problems, he runs away from problems, but never, never, never does he solve them."

He looked at her doubtfully. "But he did say he'd be down. I'd like so much to meet him." When she didn't answer, he said, "What I'd really like is to get him to come visit us in Boulder . . ."

"And fill him with Rocky Mountain air? Feed him Coors beer brewed from mountain springs and watch him purify before your eyes? Forget it. It didn't work before, did it?"

"Well, he stayed married to my mother longer than to anybody else."

"Which probably proves she took better care of him than

82

the others, made life more attractive, didn't nag at him. George Rhys . . . and I'm fond of him, you understand . . . is like a handsome colt that nuzzles your pocket for sugar one minute and spills you off and bolts the next. There's nothing on earth you can do about George Rhys."

"You're hard on him."

"No, I'm realistic about him. We've all had a go at doing something about George Rhys. It's almost a family sport. But you can never win."

He walked over to the window and sniffed at a magnolia blossom floating in a glass bowl. "Well, I'll wait and see him this weekend and then I'll take off for Colorado and stop stirring things up, leave people in peace."

"I hope you'll go in peace." She said it gently.

He went to the piano and looked at the music on the rack. "Why don't you go back to music school and study composing?"

"I might," she said dreamily. "I might."

"I talked Jordan into trying to paint after he got sick. He'd always wanted to, but he was afraid he wouldn't be any good."

"Was he good?"

"I don't know. He didn't really have time to find out. But I think he enjoyed it." He looked at her. " 'Go in peace,' you said. It sounds like a benediction."

"It is. I've grown very fond of you."

"Me too, of you." He grinned. "My mother would hate that sentence."

She held out her hand to him. "I'm very glad you came. You've been good for me in some way I don't entirely understand. I wish I could be some good to you."

He took her hand. "I think you have been," he said. "Maybe more than I've exactly figured out yet." He felt the quick tears that had threatened him so often since Jordan's death. "I'd better go. See you later." He lifted her hand, kissed it, and hurried out of the room.

fifteenth

The day woke to sweltering heat. All night thunder had rumbled somewhere to the south, and it had been too hot to sleep. Skipper went to the river early for a cooling swim, but already a dozen people were there, and during the morning he saw nearly everyone he knew going to the river, or coming home. Mary Rhys took him to a special place of hers, where there was a small cove.

"Hardly anyone comes here," she said, "except some of the children, because the bottom is so snaggy." She pointed to the big roots, some of them covered by the water, some half out. "Once you swim out a little way, you're fine, but mind the current."

He was impressed with how well she swam, and then

85

thought of his mother saying, "Why do you think no one over thirty-five can do anything athletic?"

"My mother is a good swimmer, too."

Mary Rhys treaded water beside him, shaking a silvery shower from her hair. "I'd love so to meet her."

"You must come visit us."

Later when they were walking back to the house, he said, "I'm trying to persuade my father to come for a visit."

She shot him a surprised look. "Are you sure?" Then quickly she said, "I don't mean that unkindly. I love George. But he does rile up the waters."

"That's what Mary Gwyn said. But what's to rile up?"

"It could upset your mother. Shouldn't you ask her before you urge him to come?"

"I'm sure she wouldn't care. But even if he doesn't come, won't you come anyway?"

She looked pleased. "I will. I really will. I'd like to come when there's lots of snow."

"Good. Come for Christmas."

In the afternoon he went with her to Mama-Maeve's house, taking a bowl of homemade ice cream packed in ice.

"We'd better step lively," she said, "or it will melt before we get there. But Mama-Maeve and Papa-Rhys do love my strawberry ice cream."

Skipper looked up as thunder boomed in the distance. "We're going to get a storm."

"I hope so. This sultry weather is unnerving."

Mama-Maeve took them into her cool living room, after Mary Rhys had put the ice cream in the freezer.

"Rhys will love some of that," Mama-Maeve said. "This weather affects him, poor lamb. He's feeling poorly, had a sleepless night. Before you go, Skipper, you stop in a moment and say hello."

"Me?"

"Yes. He's feeling sorry he was so cold to you. We've talked it over. He sees it's unjust."

"I'm glad. I wish he'd like me."

"He will, dear." She got a frosted pitcher of iced tea and poured out four glasses. "I'll just take him a glass of tea and let him know you'll be by to see him."

Mary Rhys nodded when Mama-Maeve was out of the room. "I thought she'd make him see. He's not an unjust man, Papa-Rhys." She picked up a bamboo fan and fanned herself. "I declare, I wonder sometimes if the *Canterbury Tales* would have turned out differently if Chaucer had lived in our climate. Would the Wife of Bath ever have left home?"

Skipper laughed.

Mama-Maeve came back looking concerned. "He really doesn't look well."

"Oh, I'm so sorry," Mary Rhys said. "Can I do anything?"

"No, honey, thank you. We can't fight old Father Time, can we." She went to the kitchen and got the pitcher of iced tea. Skipper jumped up to help her.

"My father is coming down this weekend," he said. "For sure."

"That's nice," she said, but it struck him she didn't think so. Was she afraid George Rhys's presence at Llangollen would upset Papa-Rhys? "He won't be here long," he said.

Mama Rhys looked past him. "Gerald, dear, you're just in time for some nice cold tea."

Gerald stood in the doorway. "No, thanks, Mama-Maeve. I'm going to take a shower. I've been playing tennis." He went up the stairs two at a time without speaking to Skipper.

Mama-Maeve glanced at Skipper. "He didn't mean to be rude. They're so self-centered at that age."

"That's all right," he said. "I'm self-centered myself." He took the teatray from her and carried it into the other room.

In a little while Ellie May came to the door looking upset. "Miz Phillips?" she said.

"Yes, Ellie May, what is it? Come in and have some cold tea."

"No, thank you, ma'am. Mama told me to tell you she went over to clean up Mr. George Rhys's cabin like she always does, but she couldn't do it."

"Why? What's wrong?"

"Somebody left a dead skunk on the steps."

Mama-Maeve swerved backward in her chair, as if to duck the words. "Oh dear, oh dear," she said, almost inaudibly.

"Listen," Skipper said, "tell your mother I'll deal with it." He gave her a reassuring grin. "I've run into dead skunks before. Tell her I'll clean up the cabin and get the stink out. The smell, I mean."

Ellie May looked relieved. "I'll tell her." She left quickly.

"Do you mind, Skipper?" Mary Rhys said. "That's not a pleasant job."

"Not at all." But he wasn't thinking so much of the skunk as he was of Gerald. Afraid Mama-Maeve might be thinking the same thing, he said, "Kids must have done it."

Mama-Maeve gave a long, trembling sigh. "I'm about to be too old," she said, "too old for all this turmoil." She closed her eyes. Then she opened them, sat up a little, and called, "Gerald?" There was no answer.

"Do you want us to go, Mama-Maeve?" Mary Rhys said.

"Yes, you had better go, I'm sorry. Skipper, you say hello to Rhys first, please. He's in the room at the top of the stairs."

Skipper went upstairs feeling uneasy. What if Gerald were in the old man's room? Gerald would not like his making up with Papa-Rhys. He knocked lightly, hoping the old man was asleep.

After a moment he heard bedsprings creak, and Papa-Rhys's hoarse voice called, "Come."

The room was dimmed by bamboo shades, and a big ceiling fan spun with a faint whirr. Papa-Rhys sat squarely in the middle of a four-poster bed, several big pillows propped at his back, and the glass of iced tea, partly gone, on the table beside him. He looked at Skipper, blinking his good eye, staring past him with the eye of stone.

"Good morning, sir," Skipper said, and realized it was mid-afternoon. "Good afternoon, I mean." A flash of lightning lit the room, followed in a moment by a roll of thunder.

"Six," Papa-Rhys said.

Skipper looked blank. Then he remembered, you counted slowly between the lightning and the thunder to get the number of miles between you and the lightning. He grinned. "Six miles and coming our way."

Papa-Rhys' mouth moved a little. It might have been a smile. Skipper began to relax.

"I just stopped in to say hello," he said. "I'm sorry you're not feeling good. My mother always says . . ." He hesitated. That was the wrong thing to say, but he had to go on now. "She says people are apt not to feel good just before a storm. All that electricity or something."

"She's right." Papa-Rhys said.

Skipper drew a long breath of relief. "Can I get you anything? Mary Rhys brought some wonderful ice cream. Strawberry."

Papa-Rhys's good eye brightened. "Tell Maeve . . ." He nodded.

"You'd like some. I'll tell her." Skipper went closer to the bed and looked down at this ancient man who was his forebear, his ancestor, the cause of it all. "I won't stay. I don't want to tire you." He hesitated. "I liked talking to you." Again he paused. "I'm leaving Llangollen."

Slowly Papa-Rhys put up his hand and Skipper took it. The old man didn't say anything, but there was pressure in his grasp. Skipper was moved. He wished he could think of something important to say.

There was a light knock on the door and Gerald came in, saying, "Papa-Rhys, I . . ." He stopped and stared at them in disbelief. Then he turned quickly and left. He was not in sight when Skipper came out into the hall.

Mama-Maeve looked tired and old when Skipper and Mary Rhys said good-bye.

"The woman is almost ninety years old," Mary Rhys said as they walked home. "When can she have some peace?"

The rain came in a warm pelting shower. Skipper took Mary Rhys's hand and they ran up the path to her house.

JOURNAL: It was raining when I cleaned up my father's cabin, and that made it a little easier, but removing a dead skunk, the body and the stink thereof, is not my idea of the best way to spend a few hours. I went off toting a large jug of vinegar, mops, broom, et cetera, et cetera, plus burlap bag for the remains. (Either the skunk's or mine.) The business took a while, but after some time I could take a breath without gagging. Heated up lots of water in the cabin and poured Clorox all over the steps and myself and scrubbed and scrubbed.

90

By the time I reached the indoor stage, Savannah showed up, wearing her oldest jeans and making a production of a clothespin on the nose. She really helped though, and she is good company. She said she'd been looking up how to get rid of skunk smell in a book called *The Young Housekeeper's Friend,* published in 1859. Couldn't find a thing about skunks, but she learned you can get rid of red ants by strewing oyster shells around. Very useful thing to know. Also if you have a featherbed made with new feathers and they smell bad, you put a cover on the mattress and cart it off to the baker and ask him if he'd mind sticking it into his oven when he bakes his loaves of bread. It works wonders for the featherbed, and we are left to imagine, as Savannah said, what gourmet wonders it accomplishes for the bread. Be sure your baker does this for two nights. I enjoyed Savannah because we never talked about anything even vaguely serious. She's a funny girl.

The cabin is simple but nice, all one room, everything very functional, with whitewashed walls and wide plank floors. Strange to think of it as a slave cabin. I hope the old man won't be able to detect the scent of his uninvited neighbor by the time he gets down here.

When we came out, an unpleasant note: I saw Billy John in the distance. His back was toward us and I don't know if he knew we were there. Savannah says he is a weasel, a serpent, a cretin, a monster. That about sums him up, though I think she's being a little hard on serpents and weasels. Just monster would do it.

All right, Pater, I'm ready for you. Come on down. And you'd better make it this time.

sixteenth

Skipper woke to find the rain had stopped and the air was as hot and smothering as it had been before the shower. Thunder still rumbled somewhere in the distance. He threw off the sheet and turned on his elbow to look at the luminous dial of Jordan's watch. It was not quite midnight. Eleven fifty-one, to be exact. He watched the digit change to eleven fifty-two. Twenty-three fifty-two on the twenty-four hour dial. It was a super watch. He hoped it would last him all his life.

He lay back and waited for sleep. The all-night southern heat seemed strange and uncomfortable to him. At home the nights were always cool. He longed for a glimpse of the Flatirons from his bedroom. Well, in a few days now he would be going home. To what? That was the question, wasn't it?

What he had come here to find out. And had he? Almost, he thought. Though why or what he wasn't quite sure yet.

He shut his eyes and tried to will himself to sleep, but sleep wouldn't come. If Billy John and Gerald had done that business with the skunk, and they probably had, what a lowdown thing to do. People spoke of a lowdown skunk when they wanted to speak ill of someone, but a skunk was really a very nice little animal if you didn't bother him. They must have gone out and killed one. Poor little guy. He wondered how they'd managed it without getting any of the scent on themselves. He thought of Gerald's haste to take a shower, but no, that couldn't have been the reason. They would have noticed. His haste to take a shower was an excuse to get away from his unwanted brother.

Well, he could take a hint, Skipper decided. Especially when it had been repeated about twenty times with increasing volume. Maybe when Gerald got older, he wouldn't look so much like Jordan. It would have been better if Phil, or one of the other boys, had resembled Jordan, instead of Gerald. But of course they were not closely related.

Mary Rhys said Mama-Maeve planned to send Gerald to the military school where his cousins went, as soon as Papa-Rhys died, but she wouldn't do it while he was alive. A good, tough school might work wonders.

He was dozing off at last when he heard some kind of commotion and sat up. It wasn't near at hand, but in the quiet night, sounds carried. He tried to make out what it was. He heard Mary Rhys get up and pad downstairs in her slippers. So he found the terry robe Phil had lent him for swimming and followed her. As he came into the lighted kitchen, the telephone rang. And at the same moment he smelled smoke.

Mary Rhys listened intently for a moment, said, "Oh, dear! All right," and hung up. She turned to Skipper wide-eyed with dismay. "George Rhys's cabin is on fire."

Skipper ran down the dark path in the woods, his robe flapping. He could hear the fire engine wailing in the distance, and ahead of him in the dark he saw the flicker of flashlights. As he broke out of the woods, he saw the cabin blazing. He passed Uncle Adam, who was hurrying along in his pajamas, with Phil and young Adam close behind. Jim Charles was already there, looking like a bespectacled stork in his bathrobe and his long bare legs and rumpled crest of hair. His son Chick caught up with them and said, "How did it happen?"

Jim Charles looked from one to the other. "Who knows."

The fire hose was spraying the cabin now but it was clear that nothing could be done. Lightning streaked the sky as if in reflection of the flames.

Uncle Adam touched Skipper's shoulder and said, "Don't worry. I'm sure George had insurance."

"As a matter of fact, he didn't," Chick said.

"Well, no bother about that," Uncle Adam said. "We'll look after it."

"I just wonder how it happened," Jim Charles said.

One of the firemen came around the corner of the cabin carrying something. The light of the fire turned him red. "Here's your answer." He held out a kerosene can. "Still half-full."

"Skipper," Uncle Adam said, "you kids didn't use kerosene, cleaning up after the skunk?"

"No," Skipper said. "We used vinegar and Clorox and that kind of thing."

"Thought so."

94

"Set then," Jim Charles said. "Who would do such a thing?"

There was a moment of tight silence, as if no one wanted to think of answers to that question.

"Vandals," the fireman said. "We had a case over to Fayetteville . . ."

Skipper turned away and went back along the dark path to Mary Rhys's house. He was drinking some of the coffee Mary Rhys had made when Phillip knocked on the door. He put an envelope on the table. "They collected some money for George Rhys. It ought to cover rebuilding, they said." He seemed a little uncomfortable.

"Thank you, Phil," Mary Rhys said, "that was thoughtful. Will you have a Coke, dear?"

"No'm, thank you. I got to go." He looked at Skipper. "Somebody said he was coming down this weekend . . ."

"Yes, he was."

"Dad thought maybe you would want to call him. If you don't want to, he will."

"I'll call him."

"Right." He started for the door.

"Phil," Skipper said, "are you playing tennis with Gerald in the morning?"

"Yes."

"Will you ask him to meet me down by the river, maybe around eleven?"

Phil looked a little frightened. "Yeah, sure, I'll tell him."

"Thanks."

When he had gone, Mary Rhys said, "Phillip is a good boy." But her voice was faraway, as if she were not thinking of Phil.

Skipper said good night and went to bed.

seventeenth

In the morning Skipper called his father and told him about the fire. There was a long silence, and then George Rhys said in a tired voice, "So that's that."

"Mary Rhys said for you to come on down and stay with her, and Aunt Gwyn said the same. The place isn't totally destroyed, and the family put up money to rebuild it. It wasn't insured, was it?"

His voice sounded far away. "Who insures slave cabins?"

"Well, anyway, you'll be able to see what needs to be done."

"I don't think I'll come down, Skipper."

Skipper caught his breath. "Not come down? Not at all?"

"Why should I? There's nothing there for me."

Skipper wanted to say, "There's me, for starters," but he didn't. "I'm sorry I won't see you," he said. "I'll be leaving."

George Rhys's voice perked up a little. "Say, I'm sorry too, but we'll make it one of these days. I may surprise you and show up in Colorado."

Hope leaped up and died down again. "If you come," Skipper said politely, "we'll be glad to see you."

"Right-o then, have a good trip home. Remember me to Terry and Tony and Alex. And your mother, of course."

"Sure," Skipper said.

He put down the phone and it came to him then—you made your own patterns. Nobody, no matter how close, made them for you. Mary Rhys came into the room. "He's not coming."

She gave him a quick look. "People don't always behave the way we wish they would, do they," she said. "It's a disappointment sometimes. The radio says we'll have showers this afternoon and this awful heat will break. I do hope so. Would you like your eggs poached? I have some hot biscuits, and your Aunt Gwyn sent over a jar of her apricot marmalade . . ."

He tried to be polite, but he hardly heard her, and he ate his breakfast quickly. He had overslept. He must get down to the river so as not to miss Gerald.

He was sweating and breathing hard by the time he got to the river. He plunged in at once and let the cool water relax him. He had to handle this well, not go off like a half-cocked pistol and say all the wrong things. Somebody had to talk seriously to Gerald, and he was his brother after all. But he was nervous. He tried to plan what to say, but everything that occurred to him sounded too accusing, or too uncaring. But he did care. This brother with Jordan's looks, somebody had to help him. Papa-Rhys was too old, Mama-Maeve would be ignored, the other relatives didn't seem to see him as their responsibility. Or perhaps that wasn't fair: it would take a brave soul to risk Papa-Rhys's displeasure, and Gerald would certainly run to him at once for protection. Only Billy John exerted an influence.

He turned on his back and let the current take him away. It was stronger than it looked, and the landing was already out of sight when he turned out of the center of the stream and started back.

Gerald was coming down the path in his tennis shorts, swinging his racket. He looked untroubled, even happy. He must have beaten Phil again, Skipper thought.

"Hey." Gerald came out onto a rickety little wharf that the boys had built for diving. "Still hot." But he looked cool, and his hair was combed back neatly.

Skipper pulled himself up onto the end of the wharf. His heart was pounding. "Yeah. Real hot. Radio says rain this afternoon." He tossed the water back from his hair. "How was the game?"

Gerald smiled. "Six–four, six–three."

"Poor Phil."

Gerald shrugged. "He'll learn. But he falls over his own feet."

And you never do, Skipper thought with sudden anger. You never fall over your neat, muscular, well-tanned feet. He turned to look directly at Gerald, straight at that smiling Jordan face.

"Dad decided not to come down."

Gerald's eyes brightened. "Figured he would."

"Gerald," Skipper said, "I'm your brother, right?"

Gerald laughed. "So they say."

"And I care about you, I really do."

Gerald raised his eyebrows. "Come off it. You don't even know me. You never so much as sent me a Christmas card, any of you, in your whole lives."

Skipper stared at him. "You idiot! We didn't even know you existed. You knew about us—we never heard of you."

"Oh, sure."

Skipper bit his lip. No good losing his temper right off the bat. "Well, you can believe it or not, but we did not. I'm sure my mother didn't know, either. But that's water under the bridge. I'm here now, and I've met you, and I wish we could be . . . well, at least friends."

Gerald twirled the tennis racket. "People don't get to be friends just like that, just by showing up one day and saying let's be friends."

"Well, we can begin, can't we?" Skipper's voice showed his impatience, and Gerald stiffened. "We can make a start."

"Look, Skipper," Gerald said, "the best way for us to be friends is for you to be in Colorado or wherever it is, and me to be here." He got to his feet. "Papa-Rhys doesn't like having you here. It upsets him."

Skipper stood up too. He felt the tickle of the river water dripping off his ankles. "I don't think that's true any more. I saw him yesterday. I think he's accepted me . . ."

Gerald's face blazed. "He hates your guts, and for God's sake will you get out of here where nobody wants you! You and George Rhys trying to take over . . ."

"Did you set fire to George Rhys's house?" He had never meant to say it like that, but there it was, the words like electricity between them.

99

Gerald's first reaction was fear. Skipper could see it in his eyes. Then bravado. "You're a damned liar," he said.

"Did you do it? Because arson is a crime, you know."

Gerald started to answer, but something in the river caught his eye. He was looking past Skipper at the water, and a faint grin crossed his face. Skipper turned to see what he was looking at, and Gerald gave him a hard shove with the tennis racket. Caught off-balance Skipper fell backward into the river with a great splash.

He came to the surface in a fury, shaking his head and coughing. He expected to see Gerald laughing. But Gerald wasn't laughing. He was staring intently at a place in the water just behind Skipper.

Skipper turned his head and saw a snake swimming toward him. The long black body rose and dipped in the wake of Skipper's splash. It was a thick snake, with a broad ugly head. Cottonmouth! Skipper froze for a moment and then struck out for shore. He made it in four long strokes. Scrambling onto dry ground, he looked back. The snake made its sinuous way almost to land, and then moved out again into the current, its head lifted. Then it disappeared down stream.

Gerald came off the wharf and started to pass Skipper. "It was just a little old field snake," he said.

"It was a cottonmouth, and you knew it." Skipper didn't recognize his own voice. His hands shook. "You did that on purpose. You could have killed me."

Gerald widened his eyes in innocent surprise. "You must be crazy."

"You saw that snake and you pushed me off the wharf."

"You lost your balance," Gerald said. "You fell." He grinned.

100

Skipper hit him, a hard slap on the face that snapped his head to one side. A look of surprise and then rage crossed Gerald's face. He sprang at Skipper.

The two rolled on the ground in a fierce embrace, first one, then the other gaining the advantage. Skipper threw Gerald off with a lunge of his knees and jumped to his feet. They faced each other, sweating and panting.

"Gerald," Skipper said, "this is *stupid*—"

But Gerald struck out at him with a hard blow on the jaw. Pain misted Skipper's vision, but he closed in on Gerald and backed him up against a tree. He drew back his fist for a blow to the face, but it was Jordan's face he saw and he couldn't do it. His hesitation gave Gerald a chance to wrench free and to hit Skipper hard in the stomach and shoulder. Skipper sprawled backward onto the pine needles.

He opened his eyes slowly and found that Gerald was gone. It had begun to rain. He groaned and lay still in the rain, hurting all over. And the hurt was as much in his mind as in his body. Even Jordan's face on someone else couldn't bring Jordan back. Jordan was gone. Yet what he had been was not gone, would never be. He was a part of Skipper's pattern and always would be. Jordan was a part of him because he had loved him. Gerald was not, at least not now, because there was no real bond they shared.

After a long time he got to his knees and then to his feet. The warm rain pelted him like tiny bullets. A flash of lightning and the bang of thunder hit close by. He found Phil's terrycloth robe, wrapped it around him, and walked slowly back to Mary Rhys's house. Wincing with pain he took a shower and then began to pack. It was really time to leave.

The telephone rang. It was Aunt Gwyn and she sounded

101

strange. "No," he said, "Mary Rhys isn't here. She went into town to a library board meeting."

Aunt Gwyn paused a moment and then said, "Papa-Rhys is dead."

eighteenth

Mama-Maeve had asked them to come to the little chapel after the cremation services were over. They came, all the Phillipses who were in Llangollen at the time, and some, like elderly Cousin Herbert and Amy, who had come from Raleigh. George Rhys was not there.

Skipper had seen Gerald only at a distance since their fight. No one had mentioned the fight to him, and he had not spoken of it, although the bruise on the side of his face was plain to see.

The chairs in the chapel, arranged in a semi-circle, were nearly all full. Mama-Maeve stood at the front, looking pale and small but composed. Gerald sat directly in front of her. Skipper came in with Mary Rhys and sat halfway back. It

103

was a very small chapel, built by an early generation of Phillipses for worship and for family conferences. The octagonal shape gave the place odd shadows and patches of light. Skipper tried to imagine all those long-ago Phillipses gathering here for church service, for family conferences, for crises. It was very still, and when Mamie had wheeled Mary Gwyn's chair into the area by the door, Mama-Maeve began to speak in her low, light voice.

"I thank you for coming, some of you from a distance. Rhys would be pleased." She paused for just a moment and tilted her head back. "It is a sad occasion and yet not sad. We shall miss him grievously, and yet he had a good life, full of years, in the place he loved, among the family he loved." She paused again and clasped her hands together. "I am a very old woman. I have seen many deaths, many births. Surely they are related in some serene whole that we catch only glimpses of. The Lord giveth and the Lord taketh away, but is it not perhaps that life is like the sun, always there, bright and warming, but seen only when our faces are turned toward it, when the clouds clear and the weather is fine." She stopped again. Skipper saw tears on Mary Rhys's face, and some of the other women were weeping quietly. Gerald sat like a ramrod. Out of the corner of his eye Skipper saw Billy John and Helena and their children, but he looked away quickly. He did not want to think about Billy John.

In a stronger voice Mama-Maeve said, "I should like to tell you now, while you are all here, what Rhys's wishes were. I anticipate that not all of you will be present at the reading of the will." She looked over their heads for a moment at the mullioned window near the door. "Except for a number of bequests, the bulk of Rhys's money goes in a trust to Gerald."

104

There was no expression of surprise, and Gerald's stiff shoulders didn't move.

Mama-Maeve went on. "It was his wish that at his death each of you who leases a house here should be given your house in full ownership, both the house and the land it is on."

Gerald's body jerked, as if someone had shot him. Mama-Maeve glanced at him for a moment and went on.

"Some of you may decide to sell, or your children may, and the continuity of Llangollen, which meant so much to Rhys, will be gone, but that is a chance that must be taken. He felt quite firmly that you must not be held in thrall to the past, if that is not your wish . . ."

Gerald lunged out of his chair and ran down the aisle to the door, his face contorted with tears. Everyone stirred and turned, Uncle Adam half rose, but it was young Savannah, sitting in the back near her sister, who got up quickly and followed Gerald outside. Skipper watched with more indifference than he might have thought possible three or four days before. There were some people you could help, and some people you couldn't.

In a sad, tired voice, Mama-Maeve said, "I'm sorry it's a shock to Gerald. If he had other expectations, we are at fault for letting them exist . . ."

Billy John spoke up, his harsh voice making everyone start. "I'd like to ask, please, when Papa-Rhys made this will you speak of."

She gave him a faint smile. "About six months ago, Billy John. He was in complete possession of his senses at the time. Indeed, at all times."

Billy John climbed clumsily past his wife and children and left the chapel.

Mama-Maeve lifted her hands in a supplicating gesture.

105

"Be kind to Gerald. He is disappointed. Rhys was concerned that the place should not be sold off as a development. The will, I think, is fair to all of you. If you will come now to the Old House, Sally Maeve has prepared refreshment for us."

nineteenth

Before he left for Raleigh, Skipper went out to the Phillips family graveyard with Mama-Maeve to carry some fresh flowers to Papa-Rhys's grave. He had not been there before. It was a quiet, grassy place bordered by big trees. Tactfully he left Mama-Maeve alone as she rearranged the flowers and discarded the wilted ones. The names on the old gravestones interested him, and he began to hunt for Squire Phillips. He found him at last, near the edge of the clearing, his simple granite stone slightly tilted and mossy with age. So you started it all, he thought. He bent closer to read the inscription under the name and the dates: "He sleeps peaceful in his adopted land."

Next to him was his wife's grave, and just behind them he

read the inscriptions on two small stones for a boy named James Rhys Phillips, dead at the age of three, and a girl, born two years later, also dead at the age of three. He thought how frightening it must have been afterwards until the succeeding children were past three. There was a boy who had died at Skipper's own age, apparently also a child of the Squire's, named Charles. He wondered about Charles for a few minutes. What had he been like? What had he done, what games had to liked, what brothers and sisters had he teased? How had they felt when he died?

Feeling sad he moved away and found some later members of the family who had lived to a hearty old age. In a few minutes Mama-Maeve joined him. She had made no sound of weeping, but there were tears on her cheeks.

"A lot of young ones," Skipper said. "Life must have been hazardous then."

"Life is always hazardous," she said. She carried some dead flowers to the trash can and threw them in.

"I guess we ought to be used to death," Skipper said. "I mean . . ." He gestured toward the graves. "There it is, happening every day. It's the one thing that's *bound* to happen, so why is it such a shock?"

"When it happens to *us*," she said, "it's always the first time it ever happened. Nothing prepares us, nothing."

"Not even . . ."

When he hesitated, she said, "No, not even age. Not even when it happens time after time. When you love someone, you always think, This time I won't lose him." She pointed to another grave. "Your grandfather's."

"Oh." Skipper knelt down to read the inscription, and the one for his grandmother's beside it. "I had no idea they were so young!"

"Oh, yes. Young, happy, doing what they loved." She touched the edge of her son's gravestone and turned abruptly away. After a moment she said, "Life can be very cruel, Skipper, very bitter. But there is also great joy. We must look for the joy, as long as we live. Love hurts the most, but love is what we must have, must give, or we might as well be dead ourselves." She touched his arm. "I am being a very gloomy old woman. Come walk me home, and then you must be on your way. You're sure you don't want one of the men to drive you to the airport? Chick and Jim Charles both offered, and Savannah, too . . ."

"No, I think I want to leave the way I came. Kind of under my own steam."

They walked along the grassy path in silence for a few minutes, and then Skipper said, "What will happen about Gerald?"

"I shall send him to military school."

"Military life will be a shock to him, the discipline and all."

"Yes, it will. Rhys spoiled him so. But Gerald enjoys a challenge, you know. And he does so well at everything."

"I wish we could have been friends."

"He treated you very badly. But he saw you as a threat."

"You mean that nonsense about me inheriting from Papa-Rhys?"

"More than that. The one person he has ever loved is Rhys. He was very jealous of him, even with me. Don't think too badly of him, Skipper. He suffered very much from what he saw as his father's desertion."

"It *was* desertion. My father deserted all of us."

She sighed. "Yes."

"Maybe when Gerald is older, he'll be friends with us."

"Don't count on it. In some ways he is like George Rhys;

he charms, but he seldom gives. But he has drive, which George lacks. Gerald won't make a mess of things." As they came to her house, she changed her tone. "Well, then, here we are." She took both his hands. "My dear, I am so very glad you came."

Skipper bent down and kissed her. He was glad he had come, too. He hadn't found a father, and he hadn't found a brother. But he had found people he could love—a promise in a way, for the future.

JOURNAL: I rode my bike out to the road and looked back at Llangollen, the dreaming and peaceful-looking place where half my genes come from. I smelled the pines and the flowers and all. I have found a lot of people who belong to me, that I belong to. I've made friends. I've made enemies. But I'm glad I came. I'm in the airport now waiting for the plane to take me home. This is the end of my journey and the end of my journal.

To my brother Jordan, good-bye and hello.